MW01713002

CORE SHIFTER

CHRIS HEINICKE &
KATE REEDWOOD

CORE SHIFTER

Legacy Hunter Book 6

Chris Heinicke & Kate Reedwood

Copyright © 2021 KC Stories,
Chris Heinicke and Kathryn Sherwood
All Rights Reserved

KC STORIES

This book is a work of fiction. Any references to real events, real people, and real places are used fictitiously. Other names, characters, places, and incidents are products of the author's imagination, and any resemblance to persons, living or dead, actual events, organizations, or places is entirely coincidental. All rights are reserved. This book is intended for the purchaser of this e-book ONLY. No part of this book may be reproduced or transmitted in any form or by any means, graphic, electronic, or mechanical, including photocopying, recording, taping, or by any information storage retrieval system, without the express written permission of the author. All songs, song titles, and lyrics contained in this book are the property of the respective songwriters and copyright holders. Both authors and editor have taken great effort in presenting a manuscript free of errors. However, editing errors are ultimately the responsibility of the authors. This book is written in US English, therefore, includes US diction.

ISBN: 978-1-7771102-8-4

Editing and Proofreading by Swish Design & Editing
Book Design by Swish Design & Editing
Cover Design by KC Stories
Cover Image Copyright 2021
First Edition 2021
Copyright © 2021 KC Stories,
Chris Heinicke & Kathryn Sherwood
All Rights Reserved

DEDICATION

To Alex, Ethan, Krystal, and Siobhan
May all your adventures take you out of this world
and bring you happy endings.

In loving memory of Eric Templeman
'Master Baker'
June 29, 1944 – April 13, 2020

CORE
SHIFTER

PROLOGUE

Heels clacking against the hard flooring, Rosamunde Cruz entered the interrogation room aboard her personal command cruiser, the Rose Thorn, and stared at the man she hated most in the universe.

Tobias Cruz lay on a metal examination table with his ankles and wrists restrained, which seemed unnecessary given the decrepit state of his weakened body and mind. Rose, however, wasn't one to take risks with anyone. Just because Tobias looked half-dead didn't mean he wasn't capable of screwing her over, a skill he seemed to have perfected during the past twenty-odd years of unholy matrimony. She'd wanted him tossed out the nearest airlock with the rest of the trash by now, but nothing ever went smoothly with her soon-to-be very ex-husband. Not even his death.

She placed her hands on the table's edge and

looked down at his bruised and bloodied face. “You’ve done something, haven’t you? I don’t know how, but you have.”

They had scanned Tobias’s brain and extracted his memories down to the last detail, but it seemed some inconsistencies existed. Most likely the fault of his imperfect mind, but they were going to have to be a bit more thorough now to ensure it wasn’t the result of a cognitive implant or some other trick. She wouldn’t put anything past him and the Collective.

He cracked a swollen eyelid. As his gaze focused on her, a deep rumble hitched in his chest, causing him to cough in a rhythmic pattern. A fresh trickle of blood oozed from his cracked lips as they twitched.

“Are you… are you laughing at me?”

The coughing increased, turning more into a bark. It sounded painful. *Good.* He deserved it as well as the broken ribs.

“Go on,” she said. “Have your laugh. It won’t make any difference.” She leaned down toward him. “We’ve got places. And names. So many names. Names of people who are about to die, and all thanks to you. Whether they’re the right names or not, I really don’t care anymore. Because the galaxy is going to remember that you were the cause of their deaths, and the ones who are left will cheer when they see your head in a box. They’ll finally understand what a traitor you are." She glanced at the technicians waiting nearby with their medical equipment. "Fix him up. I want his face recognizable, so there's no doubt it's him when I kill him." They could always fix the holographic imagery to be Tobias's likeness, but authenticity counted when executing a traitor for public display.

The two technicians nodded and began working on his face, using their equipment to heal the wounds and bring down the swelling. Throughout it all, Tobias stared back at Rose, calmly defiant, not making a sound. He had been handsome once, full of vigor and promise, which returned a little as the bruises faded. But he was broken now and, in that brokenness, useful to her purpose one last time.

"I should do you a favor and end your miserable existence right now after all you've given me. But I want you to see the damage you've caused before I make an example of you." She turned to the technicians as they finished their tasks and began packing their equipment. "Excellent work."

They moved aside and waited expectantly for further instructions while she inspected the results. Rose stroked her fingers down Tobias's cheek. His newly regenerated skin was smooth and warm. She touched her thumb pad to his lips, which were no longer cracked and bleeding but soft and supple. It was a shame, really, for the technicians to do such good work. He'd be dead inside ten minutes. She stood back and nodded at the nearest technician assistant, who switched on a holo emitter. The other adjusted the table where Tobias was secured, tilting the platform until it was vertical, and the failed leader of the Freedom Collective was upright. He sagged against his restraints. She grasped his hair, keeping his head from drooping down onto his chest.

"You will watch," she said. "We're starting with your right-hand man, Pion Pear. It figures you'd choose an Endarian as the first mate. Your weakness."

The feed on the holo emitter flickered to life, and a Core officer appeared on the bridge of a starship. He snapped to attention and gave a sharp salute. "Ma'am. Captain Peppard of battle cruiser Velocity-3. We've exited hyperspace at the Pendal system and scanned the area, but there's no sign of a Collective fleet. They must have flown to another system."

"Peppard, you've just arrived recently. They could be on one of the moons or any ship flying around in the system."

"We've scanned for any identifying signatures, Ms. Cruz. If they were here, they're long gone."

Rose stared at Tobias. "The information comes directly from the Collective commander himself. The traitors couldn't have gone far. Keep searching the area."

"Yes, ma'am." Peppard's expression was devoid of any enthusiasm as the holo feed cut off.

Rose paced back and forth in front of Tobias as she thought about the possibilities. She regarded his expressionless face.

"Old information to keep wasting my time?" This wasn't the first false lead they'd encountered when rounding up the Collective leaders, but whether Tobias served them false leads or not, he was a dead man. And so were his co-conspirators. "How fortunate we have more than one location targeted." She spoke into her shipboard comm and addressed her vessel's bridge crew. "How long until we reach the next targeted Collective location, Captain?"

"Less than two minutes, ma'am."

"Good." She nodded. "Perhaps there will be more of an audience at this one." Not that it mattered. She was going to record the execution and transmit it across the galaxy anyway. There was something about executing a traitor before witnesses that held great appeal, especially if the witnesses were some of his most trusted people. It was a pity that Ellie and Caree wouldn't be able to see it firsthand. But she wasn't willing to wait on their presence to end his life. The message his execution would send to the Collective supporters was too vital to wait on.

She glanced at the technicians. "Did you examine all the data extracted from Tobias's mind? If you've missed anything, there will be consequences."

"We checked and rechecked everything. Data integrity is ninety-nine percent with accuracy variance at an extreme minimum, ma'am. Further testing requires samples of his brain tissue."

She patted Tobias's cheek and smirked as she spoke to the technicians. "Well, you'll have that shortly."

Rose resumed pacing for a few seconds, her gaze fixed on Tobias. If he blinked, or responded, or even moved his eyes, she'd be satisfied with knowing he feared his imminent death. Instead, he stared back at her, almost smug in his preternatural calm and lack of regard for the situation. *Asshole.*

The floor moved beneath her feet as the ship lurched. She grasped the table for support and spoke into the comm. "Report."

"We've exited from hyperspace, ma'am. Several dozen ships are forming an armada where the Collective command vessel was supposed to be located. We're under attack."

"Then fight back!"

She frowned at Tobias. The cruiser she was on possessed powerful weapons, but they had expected to be approaching the Fiddler's Green, a mid-size cruiser commanded by Tobias's right-hand man, Pion Pear, in a surprise attack of their own. The scouts had verified the target, but it appeared they had been in error. No matter. At least they had a large audience.

She nodded at the nearby technician. "Activate the holo emitter and transmit to all nearby vessels and systems in this quadrant."

She unsheathed the knife attached to her belt and grasped it firmly, holding it up for display. A blaster would make a cleaner kill, but she wanted no questions about Tobias's death, and knives made for a better visual display. She held onto the edge of the table as the ship shuddered again.

"Citizens of the Galactic Community," she addressed the unseen masses through the holo emitter. "For centuries, we've existed together in peaceful co-existence, unified by the contract governed by the Galactic Trade Corporation..." She paused and stared into the emitter's recording device. "But in recent years, that peace has been jeopardized by the rebellious actions orchestrated by the group known as the Freedom Collective." The knife blade glinted as she twisted it before Tobias's face. "They have tried to unpin the very rules of cooperative governance we've lived by for millennia and threatened Earth's existence in the trade community as a result. They have lied, killed, and deceived many citizens in the name of misguided justice. But today..." she glanced down at Tobias and back at the emitter, "... today I bring you true justice and the rebels' reign of terror to an end."

She touched the knife blade to Tobias's throat. He seemed remarkably calm for such a monumental moment as if he accepted that his fate was in her hands, and she was his rightful deliverance. Not that it could be any other way, but still, a bit of a struggle on his part would have at least shown some damn spirit. But she'd broken that, hadn't she, just like she'd broken his body and mind. There really was only one last thing left between them.

"Tobias Zacharias Cruz." Her heart beat fast as she uttered his full name. "Under clause C42-112 of the Galactic Trade Agreement, I hereby sentence you to death by execution for crimes against the interests of the Galactic Community and for being a traitor to all of humanity." She tightened her grip on the knife. "Til death do us part," she said through gritted teeth in a low tone only he could hear. Then she brought the knife across his throat with a swift cutting action that released them both from that sacred bond in less than a second.

1

Tobias Cruz stared at the holo transmission as it played over again, unable to take his eyes off the scene he was witnessing. Morbid fascination—that's what they'd call it. It was morbidly fascinating to watch his own death play out before him in stark detail. It wasn't so much the blood and gore that he found compelling but rather the look of satisfaction on his now very much ex-wife's face as she watched the body before her die.

Figures Rosamunde would use a knife.

"Shit! Shit, shit, shit, shit," Blake Bronson said from the pilot's chair on the Queen Bohemia. He turned and gave Tobias an apologetic glance. "Sorry. You weren't supposed to see that."

Tobias managed a light shrug as the transmission cut off. Not because it didn't bother him to see his likeness executed, but because he couldn't think of any other appropriate response.

Orchestrated by Glass, his compatriot in the inner circle of the Freedom Collective leaders, the plan to let a clone of Tobias be captured by the Trade Corporation wasn't one he'd readily agreed to. He understood the need to give Rose and her conspirators false information to gain the upper hand in the war, as well as provide protection for all of them. But the plan's success hinged on Tobias remaining hidden for the past several months and allowing his daughters and everyone else in the galaxy to believe the clone inserted on Karolta was, in fact, him. The personal price of that duplicity was, and would continue to be, high. The numbness he'd experienced while watching Rose kill his clone turned into an icy chill, sharp as the knife that had sliced his duplicate's throat.

He gripped the armrests of his seat, struggling to find the calm he needed. "My daughters can't see that recording. *Ever*."

"The holographic transmission was broadcast to all sectors in this quadrant," T-183 announced in her ultra-calm cyborg voice. "It is likely that—"

"It is likely we'll die if we don't get out of this firefight." Bronson banked the ship, narrowly avoiding a collision with a Collective fighter and the swarm of ships engaged in battle. "How did we get here anyway? This isn't where we should be!"

"Never is." Bubbles shook her large Travanian head and grasped the controls before her, assisting

Bronson with piloting the vessel.

Tobias had to agree. He wasn't quite sure how much time he'd spent on the Queen Bohemia—weeks or months—but it seemed the ship steered the crew through time and space more than vice versa.

"We aren't supposed to be anywhere near Rosamunde Cruz or her fleet of Core assholes. Get us out of here!" Bronson shouted.

"And yet, there she is, sitting all pretty on her big frelling death ship, executing poor, unsuspecting clones." Marsais pursed her full lips as she studied the navigation display. "Can't we just shoot her and end this right now?"

"No." Bronson banked the ship around a group of fighters. "Killing her at this point won't end the tyranny she's started."

"I really don't like her," Marsais said. "She's very mean to everyone. She liked killing that poor clone. You could see it in how she held that knife."

"You really know how to put things, don't you, Marsais? It's a veritable gift," Bubbles said.

The Plovanian turned from where she sat at the navigation console and stared at the Travanian, her ears pointing down. As all her species were, she was beautiful with her soft patterning of fine fur and luscious body, but the expression that passed over her face enhanced the feline quality. "You can be very mean, too, Bubbles. You should remember whose side you're on."

"The important thing is that the plan worked, and Rose thought it was the real Tobias," Bronson interjected.

"Unfortunate if you happened to be the clone, however." Tobias shook his head. Had the clone ever known he was a duplicate? Probably not, or the ruse would've been revealed as soon as Rose got into its head. The torture and pain—and every reaction to them— had to be authentic, or Rose would've suspected something wasn't right.

Glass had assured Tobias that the use of the replacement was necessary for the greater good of their cause. But was the copy of himself worth any less just because it had been manufactured? At what point did one lose objectivity and become like Rosamunde, consumed with a goal at the cost of one's humanity?

"Course plotted to the next tesseract forming in thirty-five space klicks," Remler announced.

"You could always leave me here," Tobias said. "Get me onto Rose's ship, and we can end this charade right now."

"Can't," Bronson replied. The display he was watching was flashing red. "If we let the real you get captured and tortured now, then none of us will make it out of this conflict alive, including your daughters."

"Aaand there she goes." Marsais shook her head

at the display. "Rose just jumped to hyperspace."

"Captain." T-183 turned to Bronson. "The Trade Corporation command vessel has left this system, but their fighters are still present."

"Figures." Bubbles snorted. "She ran away and left them behind to do her dirty work. Coward."

"Well, they won't last long out here without backup. The Collective fleet will make quick work of them. And we're not getting into it," Bronson said. "Stay on course for the tesseract. We need to get Tobias out of here and somewhere safe for a bit longer."

Tobias focused on Bronson. "A bit longer?" What the frell did that mean?

"Core ships approaching on starboard. Three-point-five space klicks and closing," T-183 announced. "Five fighters and one attack cruiser."

"An attack cruiser?"

"It appeared after Rose ran away."

"I don't like the looks of that." Bronson studied the viewscreen and the dreadnaught class Core vessel, which dwarfed the fighters attempting to surround it. "Remler?"

Remler shook his head as he scanned the multiple realities that were forming simultaneously on his holographic console. "Not good, boss. That cruiser is a problem."

"Right." Bronson frowned. "Marsais, Bubbles, to your gunner stations, and when you get there, concentrate your fire on that attack cruiser."

"You're going after it?" Bubbles asked as she unbuckled her restraints and began to head toward the gunner section with Marsais. "I thought you said we weren't getting involved in this fight."

"We're quicker than it, and it needs to be taken out before it takes us out or any more Freedom Collective ships." Bronson increased thrusters, and the view out the main screen became a blur of light streaks and careening ships.

"Attack cruiser has sent a missile after us," T-183 said.

"That didn't take them long." Bubbles growled as she exited the cockpit. "If we survive this, I want out of the crew."

Bronson laughed. "Just like the last time, yeah?"

"Countermeasures fired," T-183 announced. "No effect, Captain."

"Estimated time until missile impact, thirty seconds," Remler said.

"That's plenty of time," Bronson replied. "We can use this."

"You're the craziest pilot I've ever known," Bubbles yelled.

Bronson shrugged and banked the Bohemia toward the cruiser. "I may be crazy, but we're all still alive."

Tobias watched the main viewscreen. The Core vessel's multiple cannons appeared in place of the diagnostics screen that had displayed the cruiser's schematics.

"Twenty seconds," T-183 said.

"It's not just a threat this time," Bubbles screamed. "I want off this ship!"

"Stop yelling. I'm trying to focus," Marsais shouted over the shipboard comm.

Tobias gritted his teeth. It was always like this on the Bohemia. The crew was undisciplined, unprofessional, and completely misfit as a team. But it was that self-same misfit quality that seemed to be their saving grace. Bronson was either a brilliant strategist or the luckiest sonofabitch who ever lived. Tobias hadn't figured out which yet. And although he had faith in the tactic Bronson was currently using to help the Collective fighters, he saw an immediate danger. The Core fleet could target them, and despite Bronson's assurances otherwise, they could be caught by Rose's web of spies. The Bohemia was unique for a Queen-class vessel, and its ability to travel between dimensions and timelines would be of particular interest to Rose—and disastrous to everyone else—if she ever got her hands on it. Not to mention what she'd do to the crew.

"Fifteen seconds," T-183 said.

Bronson swung the ship sideways, dodging laser fire from the cruiser's cannons. The deadly bolts sailed by the Bohemia harmlessly, but the roll took them close to a small defensive tower near the center of the cruiser's top.

"Ten seconds."

Bronson sent the ship on an opposite roll, this time turning it wing over wing three times to dodge more fire. Marsais and Bubbles fired, taking out several auto cannons even with Bronson's erratic maneuvers.

"Five."

"You suck, Bronson!" Bubbles shouted.

"Only on your mother's very fine pair of..." Bronson muttered the last word under his breath as he sent the ship into an almost ninety-degree climb back in the direction of the cruiser's control tower. The Bohemia headed straight for the apex. Several Core officers were viewable through the tower windows, their terror clear as they stood at their posts, watching the Bohemia speed toward them.

Tobias tensed. Was Bronson trying to ram the cruiser? Even with its temporal shielding and unique modifications, Tobias doubted the Bohemia would survive the impact any more than the cruiser would.

Bronson slammed the steering controls upward and dodged the tower, banking so close to the shielding that the pale blue glow was visible, and the ship began to sing with the sound of over-stressed ions. The trailing missile didn't alter its course to follow. Instead, it continued straight, its velocity and size allowing it to pass through the shield barrier and make a direct hit on the cruiser. The tower bloomed in an orange glow of plasma that spread outward to neighboring parts of the cruiser.

"The Core cruiser's weapons systems have been disabled, but communications are still operative," T-183 said.

Bronson nodded. "Don't destroy it. Leave it for the others to take care of. Let's see if they can capture some Core officers alive."

"Uh..." Remler studied the temporal incursions as realities decayed and new ones took their place, a frown creasing his brow. He shook his head. "I'm... I'm not sure..."

"It's a good idea," Tobias finished for him. "If the ship can be salvaged, the Collective can use the cruiser to infiltrate the Core." He leaned forward in his seat toward the floundering ship displayed on the viewscreen. "Target the main engineering section. It needs to be disabled before they activate the self-destruct sequence..."

Bronson, Remler, and T-183's displays all flashed red simultaneously, and a proximity alert began to sound.

"The Core cruiser has activated a self-destruct sequence," T-183 confirmed. "Collective fleet is abandoning the fight and heading to the jump point.

Several Core fighters are in pursuit."

"Frell." Tobias sat back in his chair and watched the cruiser burn and Core escape shuttles ejected from its command deck. The dreadnaught would've made a valuable asset to the Collective's cause.

"Then we'd better get the frell out of here too." Bronson frowned at the Core vessel on the viewscreen. "We don't want to get caught in the blast when that thing goes boom."

As she re-entered the cockpit and took her co-pilot's seat, Bronson pointed at Bubbles and snapped his fingers as if he'd had a sudden epiphany. "We can use the slip drive! It will get us to Arfustor's place almost instantly."

"I'm not using that frelling thing in the middle of these ships. We could end up slipping up the ass of a shit-gibbon Core fighter."

Bronson smirked. "Really? I think you just don't want to see your boyfriend again so soon."

"He isn't..." the Travanian began, then stopped and shook her head as she refastened her restraints. "You know, I'm not even going to bother with this conversation because you're purposefully acting like a dick, Captain. Respectfully, of course, Captain."

"Of course." Bronson's smirk turned into a full-blown grin. "It's all about the 'D.'"

"The Arfustor tesseract is forming straight ahead," Remler announced.

The viewscreen lit up with a swirling rainbow of colors that formed around a fixed point in space directly on their current heading.

"Well, would you look at that? Right on schedule." Bronson turned to Tobias. "Damn, I'm good. Next stop, Arfustor's place."

"You said that at the last tesseract," Bubbles declared in her usual, unimpressed tone.

"Well, this one is the right one this time." Bronson glanced at Remler. "It *is* the right one this time. Right?"

Remler gave a non-committal nod of his horned head. "All things being relative, yes."

Tobias gripped the armrests of his seat. Who knew where they would end up next? An uninhabitable planet? The middle of a black hole? Or even Rosamunde Cruz's personal fleet of dicks. Traveling through dimensions in this ship seemed more of a roll of the dice than an exact science. He was looking forward to getting off and back to his life's normal flow.

But as the bright light of the tesseract surrounded the ship, one thought caught his mind.

What the frell is an Arfustor?

Gray fog, dank and clinging like a wet blanket, filled the space outside the ship as far as Tobias could see. He shivered as he turned in a small circle, trying to make out something within the gray besides the darker gray outline of the Queen Bohemia, barely discernible even just a few feet away. In the end, he gave up and focused on Bronson beside him. "This is Arfustor?"

The dark-skinned man let out a short laugh and slapped Tobias's back. The sound of his gloved hand hitting the protective exoskeleton suit was swallowed by the mist. "Arfustor? Nooo, no, no, no, no. This…" Bronson spread his arms wide and gave a quick bow, "… is the only place in this part of space to get a proper pint. Or at least it used to be. That…" he pointed into the softly swirling mist to the left of them, "… is where Arfustor likes to hide from life. But don't tell him I said that. Yeah?"

"Er… sure."

Bronson set out into the mist, Marsais and Tobias following, their footfalls as they walked along a cobble stone path the only discernible sound.

"So, Arfustor is a guy?"

Marsais shook her head. "Oh, no. He's much more than just a guy. He's a Master Baker."

She said it with such awed reverence that Tobias felt he must be missing something, a feeling he was becoming used to the more time he spent with the crew of the Bohemia. “A Master Baker? What’s a Master Baker? I’m not familiar with that species.”

“Oh, he’s… well, I’m not sure what species he is. But wait until you taste his do-nuts.” Marsais clasped her hands together and held them to her chest as if she were swooning over the prospect.

Bronson clapped Tobias on the back again. “You can stay with him until it’s time to bring you back.”

Tobias paused mid-stride. “I’m staying here? Wait. Back for what?”

Bronson grinned. “You know how this works, no spoilers.”

“No spoilers, but you could at least tell me why we’re here.”

“In good time.” Bronson smiled. He was always doing that, smiling as if the universe was some never-ending joke, and Tobias was beginning to think it didn’t mean the friendly gesture of reassurance it did for everyone else. Bronson set off forward again, followed by the others, forcing Tobias to do the same or risk getting swallowed alone by the mist.

As they continued to walk in silence, Tobias began to make out the faint outline of a round stone hut in the thinning mist ahead. Like a scene out of a documentary about ancient Anglo-Saxon Earth civilization, a thatched roof sat upon the stone building, smoke drifting lazily from a chimney. The scent of woodsmoke reminded him of hot cider and honey drizzled over a slice of freshly baked bread, though he couldn't imagine where he'd ever had either. Certainly, he'd never been here before. From somewhere to the left, a chicken clucked.

A breeze stirred the air, scattering the gray, and the blurred outlines of many shapes sharpened into fine details. Several huts, similar to the first, lined the cobbled roads at irregular intervals. Lush grasslands surrounded the buildings, extending from the village in every direction, broken by thickets of trees and hills in the distance. Calm. Peaceful. Wherever the frell he was, it was certainly very idyllic, which might be nice if a person liked idyllic.

"I think I'm going to get bored very quickly," Tobias said. What the hell would he do in this village? He had fleets to command, an ex-wife to topple from her position of power, and—

"This is our stop." Bronson nodded at the first hut they had been able to discern through the fog.

"You're leaving me here? Why? What's going on, Bronson?"

"Tobias, you and I go way back." Bronson put his hand on the metal handle on the door. "Trust me when I say you'll be safer here than with us."

"But why here?" Tobias asked. But his question was swallowed by Bronson thrusting the door open.

"Oy! Don't yer ever knock?" a deep voice boomed

out from the darkened room beyond.

Bronson spread his arms wide as he stepped inside. “Arfustor, you know I don’t like to draw attention to myself when I come here.”

Tobias stared at the unusual being who stood behind a counter in the hut. He’d never seen a species quite like this in all his travels across the galaxy. Arfustor stood at just over a meter and a half in height, with a stocky build and thick arms and legs covered with a pair of roughly spun wool hose and a tunic that stopped at the creature’s thick neck. Two pairs of eyes studied him—one pair on the end of stalks that extended a foot above Arfustor’s scaly neck and a second pair halfway down his face framed by thick glasses.

Arfustor’s nose wrinkled. “Who’s this, then? And where’s me girlfriend?” The eyes on stalks jerked as they gave Tobias a thorough once-over while the spectacled eyes turned to Bronson.

Bronson gestured in introduction. “Tobias Cruz, Commander of the Freedom Collective, and professional revolutionary. Tobias, this is Arfustor, the Master Baker of Mid-evil. Oh, and Bubbles is with the ship.”

Arfustor tutted. “Blimey! I was hopin’ to spend some time with ‘er again. That big head of ‘ers and sharp tongue… mmm.” He leaned forward and folded his meaty arms on the wooden counter in front of him. “So wot’s it now, Bronson? I know yer not 'ere to say 'hi, how's it going, old buddy,' or to go fer a pint at the Carrot and Bunny. Yer wantin' somethin'."

"Well, I was getting to that. Tobias is a very important person in the galaxy beyond. And we need to keep him here for a bit, out of the way of things."

"Oy, babysittin' duties. How often does he need his diaper changed?" Arfustor asked with a smirk.

"Every two hours, or hourly if I'm drinking beer," Tobias snapped back.

Marsais giggled. She pointed at a rack of round buns with holes in the center that were cooling in a rack near the window. "May I?"

"Help yerself, beauty."

She took one and bit into it with her tiny white teeth. "Mmm." Her eyes rolled back in her head as she licked her lips. "Oooh, my frell. I've missed this. Best in the galaxy."

"Made with the last of the good stuff I'd been savin'." Arfustor smiled, took a small square basket from beneath the counter, and began to place several of the baked goods into it. He winked at Marsais. "But a little birdie told me yer might be comin' today."

Bronson patted Tobias on the shoulder. "You don't want to drink the beer in this village right now, it's, er, missing something."

"Yer makin' fun of our predicament?" Arfustor asked.

"No." Bronson reached into his waist pouch and brought out a bag. He placed it on the counter and pushed it toward Arfustor. "You wouldn't think I'd ask for something without offering a handsome payment, would you?"

Arfustor smiled. He opened the bag and sniffed the contents. All four of his eyes opened wide with surprise. "Hops almighty! Now where in the tit-lovin' universe did yer find pure yeast?"

"Let's just say it wasn't in this one."

"Hold on. We're in a different universe?" Tobias asked.

"Well, it's more like a universe inside our universe, only this one is very small and kind of pocket-like," Bronson clarified. "And in this place, yeast is a rare commodity. So, I stop by every once in a while, to even the odds for Arfustor."

"Isn't that illegal? Meddling in the events of different realities?"

Bronson shrugged, which didn't bolster Tobias's confidence in the matter one bit.

"Well, yer keep bringin' me gold like this, and yer friend can stay 'ere as long as he likes."

"Excellent." Bronson grinned. He turned to Tobias. "You'll be safe here. We'll be back for you at 22:37 in…" he glanced at a device strapped to his wrist, "… five days. Give or take."

"That's very precise." Tobias frowned.

"Time always is."

The solemn way Bronson spoke made Tobias pause. "I really don't understand."

"It's better that you don't." Bronson looked Tobias in the eye. "We're so close to getting this whole damn thing finished, as long as we stick with the plan. Stay put here, relax. Learn how to bake do-nuts."

"Do-nuts? You can't be serious."

"Arfustor will show you," Bronson said. "He's a Master Baker." He released his grip on Tobias and turned away. "See you in five days."

"Give these to me Bubbles, aye?" Arfustor passed the basket to Marsais. "Tell 'er she needs to come see me in person next time. I'd like to show 'er what a Master Baker can do with his hands."

Marsais's mouth dropped open as she glanced at the basket and then back at Arfustor. "She's sooo frelling lucky."

"Let's hope we all are," Bronson remarked as he and the Plovanian slipped out the door and back into the thickening mist.

Tobias stared after them, filled with a deep sense of unease and the nagging question of just what he'd gotten himself into. When or if he'd ever see the crew of the Queen Bohemia again? Or his daughters?

2

Axel walked through the forest, picking his way between trees and shrubs and body after body of fallen Collective supporters. Rose's forces had struck the planet of Skasgard hard, her Core vessels firing on the helpless citizens of the capital city who had not been safe even in their homes. In the forest, they hadn't stood a chance.

The smoke of burning brush was thick, obscuring his vision. He coughed, choking on the mixed scents of burning wood and things he'd rather not think about. Somehow, somewhere, he'd lost his head gear. And his protective enviro-suit. And his guns. Barefoot and wearing only a thin t-shirt and shorts, he made for a clearing where the smoke seemed thinner.

It, too, was strewn with bodies, fallen where they'd been cut down by laser fire—young, old, civilian, soldier—so many people slain for the crime of wanting to be free of tyranny. Axel stepped carefully, looking for familiar faces but not wanting to find any.

How had this happened?

So many, so many dead.

He stopped as he recognized a bearded man.

"Kendrick?" What was his brother doing here? He looked asleep, lying curled up on his side amongst the others. He'd been at the Terra stone mine near their family home back on Earth, which wasn't anywhere near Skasgard. Or was this Earth and not Skasgard? The scorched landscape could be either. He brushed dirt from Kendrick's face. His brother's skin was cold, his pulse non-existent.

Axel bowed his head and closed his eyes. The weight of the war casualties bore down on him, causing a mixture of bile and pain to rise inside him. He clenched his fists, aching with the need to kill Rosamunde Cruz with his bare hands. She had done this—stripped these people of their lives for no reason other than she could. How could it be possible for someone as exceptional as Ellie to come from the womb of someone so evil?

A breeze blew, swirling the smoke around him and brushing his fingers with ash. He stood and walked further through the smoke and carnage. What had once been a thriving landscape had been replaced by piles and piles of bodies covered in gray ash. A swatch of color caught his eye, standing out amongst the gray. The remains of an older man and woman lay fallen together, curled in an embrace. The design of the woman's dress looked familiar. Her hair. Her ring.

"No." He moaned out loud. "No, no. no. Oh, please no."

He bent down and brushed aside the hair covering the woman's face. Tears clouded his vision as his mother stared straight at him through familiar eyes, yet vacant of recognition. The body entwined with hers was also devoid of life. His father had perished too.

"It's not real. Don't get fooled by what you see." Uncle Henry's words of warning echoed through his mind.

But when had the old man said that? Axel looked around at the expanse of gray ash. The burning and decay looked real. Felt real. Smelled real. All the death, the burned bodies and destroyed lives, and the endless aching sorrow and despair it inspired. If this was a dream, it was an extremely vivid nightmare.

"Axel?"

He glanced in the direction of the familiar soft voice.

Caree placed her hand on his shoulder. He stared at her full breasts and thighs. Her naked skin was so pale that the blue had faded to gray like the ash covering her and the world around him. Tears made tracks on her cheeks.

He pulled her toward him and wiped her tears with his palms, remembering the feeling of her soft body straddling his while he'd been near death once. Her warmth and how she was so full of life had brought him back. But now, she felt cold beneath his hands like the thousands of corpses around him. And he felt dead inside.

"I found Ellie," she said. Her words tickled his ear, her icy breath causing him to shiver.

"Ellie? But she wasn't supposed to be here." Ellie had been commanding a fleet of Collective and Resistance fighters in an attack against her mother.

"She's gone. Just like Kendrick." Her lips touched his neck, soft and supple but so cold. So cold.

"Axel, I need you to help me," Caree pleaded. She clutched at him, raining her lips over his neck and chest as she fell to her knees before him. His clothes were gone, and he was covered in ash—the gray ash of the dead.

"I need you to love me now."

Her lips touched his skin, her fingers his thighs. But there was nothing there that stirred him. She was beautiful. Sensual. Had he dreamed of her like this? Once, perhaps. Idle fantasy. But now he was ice and ash. And his heart's name was sorrow. His family. Ellie. Were gone.

"Don't you want me?" She stared up at him, her large eyes filled with emptiness, yet hungry with pain he couldn't heal.

He shook his head as he touched her hair. It floated away beneath his fingers like wisps of smoke in the wind. He stared after it as it dissipated and joined the endless gray. The wind blew stronger, and she disappeared into it, like her hair. A swirl of smoke that had never existed.

He blinked as the realization settled, releasing the chill that had him in its tight grasp. It wasn't true. Not any of it. Caree. Him. The dead. It was all an illusion. "This isn't real. I'm not really here." He glanced around him at the gray. He'd seen that gray before. Endless plains of clay. "This is a trick from the mind-eaters."

Something hit him square in his back, knocking him to the ground. His face hit a pile of ash, and he choked as he tried to breathe. He rolled to the side and wiped his face.

"This is all your fault," a gruff voice said from above him. A heavy boot connected with his shoulder, turning him onto his back. Hendrix stood over him.

"What the hell?"

The shifter picked him up from the ground and held him with a fistful of Axel's flight suit in his grasp. Axel grimaced, wondering when the nightmare would end. But at least he had clothes on again.

"You gave everyone hope, but they're all dead.

The Collective, Resistance, and even my people," Hendrix said. "You're gonna pay for this."

"But you aren't even here!" Axel shouted. "You abandoned us!"

The nightmare wasn't real, but he doubted that it would make the pain any less from the long blade that the shifter sliced through the air toward Axel's abdomen. The mind-eaters appeared to like feeding off pain and fear the best, probably for the intense emotional reaction they caused. He braced for the force of the impact, but as Hendrix's fist connected with him, the blade disappeared.

Axel glanced around the dimly lit room he now sat in. The familiar ring of faces—Ellie, Shiznit, Kendrick, Uncle Henry. All of them slumped against the wall in the lab belonging to the gray aliens on Amasis. But not Hendrix or Caree. Or the baby. What had happened to them? How long had he been here now? He had no way of knowing. There were moments like this with a glimpse of reality before being plunged back into the nightmares again. Too weak to fight. To escape.

Shiznit shifted, the sound loud in the small room. The Gho'bar moaned and shook his head, his eyes closed. "Just leave me attached. I can take it," he mumbled.

"Yes, but for how long?" Ellie asked beside him. She reached sideways, her eyes wide but not seeing the room around her and patted the fur near his horns. "I don't want you hurt."

The Gho'bar smiled, and Axel remembered what Shiznit had told him about how he enjoyed having his horns stroked.

"Just be careful there, or else he'll be wanting more," Axel said.

Ellie giggled, and her eyes drifted closed, lost in whatever illusion she shared with Shiznit. Then her face went slack, and she let out a soft sigh. "I really think I'd better get dressed now, Axel." She laughed again, this time the throaty purr he knew so well from sharing her bed.

And the reaction he'd not been able to achieve with Caree gripped him instantly.

Except he couldn't touch or reach Ellie. He could only sit there naked, chained to a wall by his wrists above his head while she sat there so close. He could smell her perfume, feel her dark hair loose and flowing, see her pale skin flawless in the dim light and her naked body, curvy and strong. Just the two of them now chained together in the room but kept apart.

But maybe that was part of the nightmare.

3

Neelix Nebula, Pelukan System

White streaks of starlight. The gut-punch sensation of shifting velocity. The familiar bitterness of bile at the back of his throat. Hendrix ticked off his mental checklist, confirming that, yes indeed, the Queen Phoenix, as Caree called their current vessel, had successfully completed the exit from hyperspace. The transition was unremarkable in every way, just like the many thousands of times the shapeshifter had experienced it during his long life cycle.

There should be something more, though, shouldn't there? he thought as he checked the readouts on the ship's monitors. When one's journey comes full circle, shouldn't something be there to mark the moment? But nothing greeted him in this sector of space except the familiar swirling haze of gas and dust that made up the

Neelix Nebula.

He mentally shrugged. What had he expected? A frelling party? He was getting soft. He'd spent too long in human form. He'd been 'Hendrix' for the greater part of five Earth years now, give or take moments when he had found it useful to be someone or something else. And his limited Homosapien brain was generating defective thoughts.

The nebula was just as it should be, unchanged since he'd last visited it nearly two Earth centuries ago. It was also uninteresting in every way, except for the amount of gamma radiation produced by several globular clusters inhabiting the same area. This made the nebula ideal for hiding things that a person didn't want to be easily detected by a scanner.

"There's nothing here," Caree said. She sat beside him in the co-pilot's chair, her blue skin pale in the cabin lighting. A slight frown pulled at her lips as she glanced at him. "No Core ships or… anything. The only thing I sense here is your fear."

"I'm not afraid."

"Yes, you are. You're worried about what will happen when we awaken your people. Phoenix senses it too."

Hendrix focused on checking the readings as he piloted the Queen Phoenix deeper into the nebula toward the exact coordinates he needed. The half-human, half-Endarian empath unsettled him. There was no way around it. Caree had always made him uneasy with her ability to sense things and the way she seemed able to see right through any bluff. But the baby, who was strapped in a seat nearby and sleeping peacefully despite the shift from hyper-speed to normal space-time, disturbed him more.

Of all the species he'd encountered, he'd never found one who was part Stardrive. Stardrive energy was a source of food for his kind. It was also very rare. And while other energy sources would sustain him, they wouldn't do so forever. Only Stardrive energy replenished him. It allowed him to grow and thrive, but more importantly, it allowed his kind to breed. And without it, his species wouldn't survive. He'd spent the greater part of his existence trying to find one—just one—to revive the last of his people. He'd come close many times to achieving his goal, then opportunity was snatched from his grasp. But now, he had what he needed to begin the process of rebuilding a place for his people in the galaxy, and it sucked its thumb while it slept, smelled like a floral nightmare, and drooled.

He glanced at the child. Had fate intended for Phoenix to be the solution to all his problems or had that been a random chance? *Fate doesn't exist, you dumbass,* he admonished himself. *There is no such thing as divine coincidence, only probability and the universal law of attraction, which follows the path of least resistance on a quantum level. I needed a power source to save my people, and the universe provided one.*

The child was a natural adaptation of human, Endarian, and Stardrive. It was an energy-based being in humanoid form, which made it adaptable and able to interact with anthropomorphic species in a way the bio-mimetic energy globes couldn't. But it possessed enough Stardrive qualities to serve his purposes. It seemed to feed incessantly, draining its mother when not sleeping, and had already grown three times its birth size in the past few days since they'd escaped Amasis. It appeared now like a human toddler more so than an infant, and it was gaining in physical strength as well as mental ability at a rate Hendrix found unnerving. What would it be once it matured?

Being around the child made him feel unstable, as if his atoms could fly apart if he let them. Stardrive was one of the few forms he could never morph into simply because their energy was so all-consuming, he'd have been burned up if he'd ever tried. It was the same with the child, but this baby was the key to his future.

"We'll be returning to Amasis to free the others once we've awakened your people, won't we, Hendrix?"

"Of course." He avoided looking at Caree and

focused on the viewscreen. He didn't need to see her to know she was questioning his motives. Her distrust of the situation had been apparent since he'd first convinced her of the need to leave Axel and the others behind so they could get help to free them. He couldn't blame her. He wouldn't trust himself either if he were in her position. He'd done a lot of things he wasn't proud of to get to this point, and she knew it. And once his people were awakened, she and her child would be outnumbered, leaving her in a vulnerable position. But he had no intention of kidnapping her baby as the aliens on Amasis had tried to do. The mind-eaters were more of a threat than she understood or remembered.

"Why did we have to leave them behind again?"

"The grays have them held captive, and there were too many mind-eaters for us to fight alone."

"Mind-eaters?"

"Yes. Remember? The assholes who feed off your mental energy and frell with your head by making you forget they exist?" She'd forgotten them again, though her mind had held onto the idea longer this time. But the constant need to remind her of what had happened was becoming beyond annoying.

"Oh. Right… oh, yes! We need your people to help us fight them. Your species is their natural enemy."

"Yes."

"But why is that?"

"In my natural state, my mind isn't the same as yours. I don't retain memories the same way. My species remembers who the mind-eaters are, and that threatens them. So, they try to kill us, and we try to kill them."

"Okay." Caree scanned the viewscreen. "But where is your ship? This is the same nebula that the Core searched, but they only found a decoy ship. Right?"

"Yes."

"Rosamunde Cruz wasn't happy."

"Yeah." He smiled, remembering how pissed the CEO of the Cruz Galactic Trading Company and Earth's representative to the Galactic Trade Corporation had been when she'd found that what she'd thought was a real ship was just a simulation. "Rosamunde Cruz is a double-crossing bitch who wants to enslave my people. She can go fuck herself." There was no damn way he'd ever let anyone find the ship that the last of his kind called home, least of all a power-hungry psychopath like her.

"Language," she said with a scowl and a glance at the sleeping baby. "He picks up things very quickly."

Hendrix managed to contain his eye roll, but just barely. The baby couldn't even talk yet, but Caree was quickly turning into a prissy mother. "You're certain you can sense nothing out there?" he asked her. He halted their forward momentum and checked his scanner readings. No other ships were around them, but he needed to be sure with the gamma radiation causing interference. He wouldn't put it past the Core to have a few ships in the nebula still scanning for any clues to where his ship might be located.

She nodded. "This area of space is empty of intent, except yours. Are you sure your ship is here?"

"Oh, it's here all right."

He focused on morphing his suit pouch into the piece of tech he'd acquired some time ago, which he'd coded to his specific DNA. The quantum field generator was always with him, no matter what he chose to make it look like to others. He attached the palm-sized device to the Queen Phoenix's main computer console while Caree watched in attentive silence. It took a moment for the device and ship to calibrate, but only a moment.

"You just need to say the magic word to see it," he said.

"Which is?"

He stared at the viewscreen as he activated the device. "Asshole," he said with a grin.

Immediately, a bubble-like distortion in space formed ahead of them, causing the Queen Phoenix to emit proximity warnings. Hendrix shut the ship's alarms off with a quick flick of the controls.

"Really?" Caree snapped, her sharp tone directed at Hendrix. "It's okay, love. It's okay," she added in a more soothing tone as she reached for Phoenix. But even the wailing of the baby who protested the sudden disruption of its sleep cycle with angry screams couldn't tear the shifter's gaze from the semi-translucent bubble in space that filled the viewscreen.

The area of darkness shimmered, reflected light from the nebula rippling and flowing across its surface like water in sunlight. The phenomenon was beautiful, but it was the object inside it, barely discernable through the swirling barrier, which made Hendrix's human heart pump harder and the hairs on his arms stand on end. So close now. So close to finishing what he'd begun so long ago as a last-ditch effort to save his kind. His secret fear had been that he'd never see his people again. Yet here he was, separated from his ancestral ship by a thin barrier of spatial differentiation.

"You hid your ship in a subspace bubble?" Caree asked.

"Yes."

She rocked the baby gently and stared at Hendrix. "And you're the only one who knew where it was?"

"It would've defeated the purpose, don't you think, if I'd left a map of how to find it."

She let out a soft breath. “That’s either the cleverest thing I’ve heard of or the most insane. If anything had happened to you, your people would have been trapped in there.”

“If I didn’t find a Stardrive to revive them with soon, it wouldn’t have mattered anyway.” He said it matter-of-factly, but he knew by her silence as she studied him and the way her eyes widened just a bit that she felt the truth of his words and the very real desperation behind them. If he hadn’t made it back to his people with a suitable energy source, they would’ve all died whether he’d left them inside the subspace bubble or not. And the universe would have moved on without a care.

“How do we get through the bubble?” Caree asked. “This Queen-class ship we took from Amasis isn’t equipped with temporal shielding.”

“We don’t. We open the bubble and bring the ship to us.” This would risk exposing it to being discovered by the Core if any squads happened their way, but it was a risk he would have to take. There hadn’t been a lot of time to choose what ship to steal when escaping from Amasis. The important thing had been to get away before the grays took Phoenix. He turned to face Caree directly. The child was watching him, curled up in her arms while it sucked on a nutritional supplement bar Caree had given him. “You’re certain Phoenix will help awaken my people from stasis?”

She nodded. “He understands what’s needed.”

Hendrix frowned. The two Stardrives they had brought with them had expired while getting them here. The energy globes had been too weak, drained by the mind-eaters on Amasis, as all the Stardrives there were. But Phoenix was strong, and Hendrix was going to have to trust in that and handle whatever might go wrong. He was out of options.

He punched a code into the emitter, and the bubble separating them from the last of his kind disappeared, allowing his ship to return to normal space.

Caree’s drawn-in breath was loud enough for him to hear. “A Millennial ship? Your people are on a Millennial ship?”

“Yes.” There it was right in front of him, the ship he’d guarded with his life, once occupied by humans but now home to the last of his species. “We found it adrift in the Helios junkyard over six centuries ago.”

“So, you just took it over? What happened to the crew?”

“It was abandoned. According to the system data, the shields had failed during a plasma burst as the ship passed through a binary system. Most of the crew were killed instantly. The survivors didn’t last long. We needed a place to hide, and as far as that goes, it was an ideal choice. Who would look for us on an abandoned Earth vessel? We repaired what we could, including the shields. We started to think it was the answer to all our needs, but things rarely work out as well as you think."

Caree was silent for a long moment. "But I don't feel a Stardrive."

Hendrix nodded. "The Stardrive was still generating power when we found the ship. It lasted for a little while longer. It's nearly dead now."

Unfortunately, both it and the ship, including its navigation logs and comms, had been stripped by scavengers when his people had discovered its existence. It was a common misconception that Stardrives were an infinite, self-replicating power source. The bio-mimetic energy globes did expire if not cared for. They were simply long-lived, much like his own species.

But despite its rough condition, the Millennial ship had functioned well, keeping his kind in cryogenic stasis until a replacement Stardrive could be found to revitalize them.

"No wonder you seemed so familiar with Millennial ships..." Caree said. "And why you wanted to find them."

Hendrix nodded as he set a course to dock with the much larger vessel. The automatic beacon responded, which was a good sign. At least there was still enough power left on the Millennial ship to run the basic systems. "It was my best option for finding another compatible Stardrive to power this ship."

Caree pursed her lips. "But Phoenix isn't going to do that. He's just going to wake your people from stasis. Right?"

"Yes. My people will need to find a new home after this and a new source for Stardrives." Again. His home world of Triamondrias had been obliterated eons ago before his own life cycle had begun, but it felt like his species had been on the run ever since, their numbers dwindling as the millennia passed.

The baby stopped sucking on the nutritional bar and gave him a sloppy grin. "Yum," it said. It jammed the bar back in its mouth and resumed sucking.

Hendrix raised his eyebrows. "That baby just spoke. What the frell is that all about?"

"I told you he picks things up fast. He's not like a typical human or Endarian," Caree said. "He's something wonderful."

"Something weird," Hendrix muttered, but that weirdness was about to save his species if everything went as planned.

The Millennial ship loomed closer as the docking port's outer hatch filled the viewscreen. Memories of being inside that vessel loomed close as well—many discussions with his people, members of his species trying to decide how best to exist. The anger. The resentment. The panic. The need to procreate versus using what was left of the dying Stardrive to power the stasis pods on the ship. And for him to set out alone to find a replacement. That decision had not been unanimous despite his position as First and, therefore, his responsibility. There were no guarantees and many risks with such a plan, but he'd accepted them all and had sacrificed his chance at prolonging his long life so that his species might prevail.

How would his people react when he woke them after years of deep sleep? Would their memories remain fresh? Or would the effects of long-term stasis have corrupted their DNA? They'd had to take on human form to be compatible with the cryo chambers on the ship. What if they couldn't survive in any other form now?

The baby stared at him as if he knew what he was thinking. "Kid, you're way too young to understand all this."

"If you hate that I know what you're feeling and thinking, you're going to hate my baby even worse." Caree grinned. "It would be a mistake to underestimate him."

Hendrix glanced at the mush escaping Phoenix's mouth while he sucked sloppily on the nutritional bar. It was all over the kid's face and hands, despite Caree's attempts to wipe it up. *The future of my species is in the hands of a drool-covered mutant.* He sighed. "Let's just get this over with, shall we?" The shifter stood and headed for the hatchway as the docking rings between the two vessels sealed. "The longer we take, the greater the risk the Core assholes will find us. And there's not enough power left in the ship to fight them."

"Phoenix can't feel the Stardrive either." Caree followed Hendrix to the hatchway, carrying the squirming baby. "Just a whisper of something, maybe."

"Exactly." He checked the power level in his blaster rifle before slinging it over his back. He caught her wary look. "We need to be ready. Just in case."

They entered the airlock and counted down the seconds before the hatchway into the Millennial ship opened.

"Do you always expect trouble?" she asked him. "Or do you just enjoy playing with guns?"

He looked down at her. "That's a stupid question. How do you think I've managed to survive for so long in this frelling universe?"

The door released, revealing the dim passageway of the Millennial ship beyond.

"Asshole," Phoenix said and spat up on Hendrix's armored chest plate.

4

"A Millennial ship," Thalia murmured to herself. "Hidden inside a subspace pocket. That's where he's kept the last of his kind all this time." She glanced at the schematics on her wrist tracker for the umpteenth time, finding it hard to comprehend the complexity of it all. Even if anyone had somehow stumbled upon the ship in subspace, no one would've guessed an abandoned near-derelict ancient Earth vessel would ever house the last of a once-proud bio-mimetic species. She shook her head. "Hendrix is very clever, I will give him that."

'And very, very stupid leaving this place unguarded like this,' Iris replied inside the cyborg's mind. *'He's usually more cautious. I still think it must be a trap.'*

"Could be," Thalia agreed. She paused in the corridor just outside the airlock doors and checked the charges on her laser blasters. "But maybe he thought the gamma radiation in this nebula would be enough of a shield. If we hadn't been tracking him from Amasis, we would never have known it was here." She'd followed Hendrix's ship to the Millennial vessel and waited until the shifter had gone on board before making her careful approach. Like Iris, she'd expected a trap to be triggered as they'd docked at the ancient Earth vessel and boarded, but it appeared that the ship simply didn't have enough power to activate even a primitive sentry system. She reviewed the telemetry on her tracker. "The shields are still down. Weapons systems offline. There is barely enough power registering to operate life support." But other than that, it was impossible to ascertain what lay in wait in the dimly lit maze of corridors ahead.

'Hendrix will want to fix the power first so he can awaken the others.'

"Agreed." Thalia studied the ship's layout. "He will be heading to the engine room."

'He may already be there. If we want to act before the ship's systems come online, we need to hurry.'

"We should report this to Rose," Thalia said, reluctant to head alone into the darkness ahead. "We may need assistance."

'Are you serious? When have we ever needed backup?' Iris asked. *'Yes, okay, we should report it IF you want to give her exactly what she wants without keeping any leverage for you. Hasn't she always been*

looking for this ship?'

"Yes."

'*Why?'*

"To control Hendrix."

'*But why?'*

"Because she wants what he has."

'*Exactly. She wants what he's been hiding on this ship. The last of his species.*' Iris felt a pause where Thalia seemed to be thinking. '*How do you think this war will go with a shifter army at Rosamunde Cruz's beckoning*?' Iris asked.

Thalia stared at the darkened passageway, alert for any sounds. "Rose will win."

'*It will at least give her the upper hand, and it will give you and me the upper hand if we get these shifters first and take control of them. She'll have to do what we want to have them. And we can use it to get us out of this one-body-two-minds bullshit that she did to us.*'

Thalia sighed. Cyborgs were designed for duty, but this mind invader was beginning to affect her way of thinking. Her words made sense.

"Agreed, sister. But where are they?" Thalia checked the ship's layout again, searching for a likely place for countless shifters to be in hiding. "I am not picking up any life signatures." She frowned at the readings. "Not even our own. The gamma radiation in this nebula is creating interference, even on board. Or maybe it is this ship." It would make sense if the shifters had installed technology to obscure their life readings to remain hidden.

'Well, let's get moving then, lazy ass. Hendrix and the Endarian are already ahead of us. And if we wait until he's awakened his kind, we won't be able to get control without a fight.'

"Well, the two of us will have to be very careful then," Thalia said. "Fighting a pack of shifters is not in my game plan." She had become used to the pirate's presence in her mind and was willing to admit that perhaps the two of their brains put together worked better than solo. But she was still hoping they could be separated.

'But why the Endarian?' Iris asked. *'Why bring her here? And the child?'* Thalia felt Iris bristle. *'He doesn't even like her.'*

"He must need her for something. Maybe to feed his people when they wake? What do shifters eat?"

'Energy.'

"Can the Endarian give him that?"

'Who knows. But maybe if he needs it, we can get Hendrix to work with us,' Iris said.

Thalia wasn't so sure about that idea. Hendrix was on the list of Rose's most wanted and working with him wasn't on her agenda.

'Rose works with people to suit her agenda,' Iris commented.

"Of course," Thalia agreed as she moved as quickly and quietly as she could down the corridor, heading for the engine room. Just like she knew there was no way to stop Iris from reading her thoughts. But if Hendrix was a shifter and on Rose's list of perpetrators to be caught, how much could he be trusted?

Hendrix walked through an antechamber that connected several corridors on the Millennial ship, Caree and the baby following closely behind him. The three of them were headed toward the engine room where the near-dead Stardrive bled its feeble life into the ship's power relays. They moved quickly, purposefully, their footfalls the only sound in the dark. Hendrix kept his laser rifle drawn and his senses sharp. The feeling of urgency he'd had since retrieving the ancient vessel from its hiding place in subspace increased with every step. His response was heightened by the emptiness of the ghost ship that echoed with memories of his life there, but also, by the reality that until he had the shields restored, they were left vulnerable. The gamma radiation in the nebula made it difficult for anyone scanning the area to find them, and that was a protection of sorts. But it also meant that he couldn't rely on scans to alert him of intruders or hostile forces. If it weren't for Caree and Phoenix's heightened senses, they'd have been completely vulnerable. It wasn't a feeling he liked. The sooner they restored shields and woke his people, the better.

"Something's wrong." Caree's soft voice seemed loud in the quiet.

Hendrix spun and looked at her.

She stood about three feet behind him, the baby in her arms, their eyes wide and staring at him. "She's here," she whispered.

"What? Who?" He looked around the antechamber, seeking signs of trouble but not finding any. But he didn't doubt her ability to sense things he couldn't. Of all the species he could've changed into to be most useful for reconnaissance, none were equal in perception to Phoenix.

He glanced at Caree, but the place where she'd been standing was now empty except for shadows.

"Fuck," he said and closed his eyes as the cold end of a blaster pressed against the side of his head.

"Where are the others?"

Hendrix froze. He knew that voice, the crisp, almost robotic tone devoid of emotion. It was a hard voice to forget when it had tortured him without mercy at Rosamunde Cruz's bidding. He thought they'd killed that voice and the cyborg it belonged to in the Borbian prison. But apparently, he'd been wrong.

He studied her from the corner of his eyes. Yep, he knew that stance, the familiar body armor, and the cold smile belonging to Thalia, Rose's number one bitch from cyborg hell.

As she reached to grab his rifle, he squeezed the trigger, getting off a shot that went wide, but hopefully, it alerted Caree to stay away, wherever she'd gone.

Thalia pressed her blaster more firmly to his head and relieved him of his weapon. "Ah, ah, ah. So naughty. Is that any way to greet an old friend?"

"Friend?"

The pressure of the gun left his temple as she stepped back with a soft laugh. "Why not?" She shrugged lightly and gestured with her blaster at him. "Hands behind your head. Come on. You know the drill." Naturally, it was the same type of stasis gun she'd had the last time she'd tried to kill him—the same one she used to kill Iris. He swore to himself that should the opportunity present itself to kill Thalia, he'd make sure to do a perfect job of it.

He placed his hands behind his head, studying her. She must have followed him here, probably tracking him for a long time. But if she knew he was here, then Rosamunde Cruz did too. Which meant he and all his kind were soon to become extinct.

"Where are the others?" she asked him a second time.

"Others?"

Her smile was devoid of humor. "The Endarian woman and child. You did not come on board alone."

She didn't know where Caree and Phoenix were? Her scanner must not be working either. Perhaps there was a chance to escape if Phoenix could wake his kind before the inevitable Core fleet arrived.

"I don't know where they are. They were right behind me."

She cocked her head to the side as if thinking. "No matter. I have you, and you will give me what I want. If you do not, well, maybe this will help you remember what will happen." She aimed her blaster at his right foot and shot it. The numbing sensation was instantaneous as his lower limb from mid-calf to toe tips became frozen in stasis shock. He staggered and tipped sideways and would've fallen if she'd not caught him.

"Bitch." He hissed. She was strong. Her body felt firm and lean against his as she held him so close her breath tickled his lips.

"You always did know how to compliment a girl." Her eyes were dark, icy cold, her smile mechanical. But there was something human about her beneath the robotic relays of her mind, something dark and familiar in her speech, the tilt of her chin. Dominant, arrogant, possessive.

His foot tingled as the blood in his vessels flowed

through it again. She shoved him away from her toward the corridor to their left. "That was the lowest setting," she said. "If you even think about changing form to come at me or escape, you know exactly what will happen. I am faster than you. Remember?"

He righted himself and turned to face her. Yes, he did remember. He remembered how he'd felt when she'd frozen him with the damn thing over and over again. And how he'd felt when she'd used it to kill Iris.

She gestured with the gun in the direction of the darkened corridor. "Get moving before that misplaced anger written all over your face gets you into trouble. Is that what happens when you spend too much time in human form? You begin to feel like one?"

"What makes you think I give a shit what you think?" Hendrix asked.

His words were returned with another shock from Thalia's weapon, but this time the stasis blast was higher, and he landed on his back on the floor, which might have hurt except he couldn't feel anything other than the choking weight of paralysis. His breaths came in shallow rasps, and he couldn't move or blink.

Thalia stood over him and pointed the gun at his head. "I heard you are intelligent, but I am beginning to think that is far from the truth."

Hendrix stared at her as the stasis blast began to wear off. Maybe she had a point. He hadn't been very smart with this so far. She had the weapons and the upper hand. He needed to stall, give Caree time to wake his people, and secure the ship before the Core arrived.

"You're kind of cute when you pull that face," he said. "You remind me of someone human." This was true. She actually kind of did with the playful interest in her gaze while watching him right now. Her dark eyes were still cold but more aloof rather than icy. Familiar, but maybe it was just the feline grace he'd observed in most female assassins.

Her eyes narrowed. "Really? Was that supposed to be some kind of witty attempt at distracting me with sarcasm?"

"Did it work?"

Her gaze traveled over the length of him. Her lips twisted into a smirk. "No."

She moved the gun aside and held out her hand instead, helping him to stand. "We want the same thing, you know?"

"You mean, you want me to kill you too?"

She shook her head. "You always make things so difficult, Hendrix. Why is that?"

"I get bored easily?"

She prodded him with her gun toward the corridor to the left. "How about we go find the other shifters you have been hiding?"

"I don't know what you mean."

She rolled her eyes. "Yes, you do. I know everything Rose wants, and she wants this ship because it holds the last of your kind. So, you are going to get me one." Her voice changed slightly as she let out a purr-like laugh. "And then you and I are going to have a very long talk, handsome."

5

Caree cradled Phoenix in her arms and waited in the shadows of a corridor off the antechamber as Hendrix and the cyborg moved down a different hallway to the right. She hadn't dared move, barely dared to breathe in case the cyborg might hear and discover her and the baby. Phoenix had kept silent without her needing to try to hush him. He'd understood the danger. He was the one who had alerted her to the cyborg's presence in the first place. Her empathic perception was strong, but his was superior, even at the advanced age of barely two weeks old.

'Uh oh,' Phoenix's thought whispered through her mind.

"Yes, I sense it, too," she whispered back. "There's something wrong with her." Despite the obvious problem that the cyborg had managed to follow them to the Millennial vessel undetected and now had Hendrix in her clutches, there was something wrong with her. Caree had been in Thalia's presence before, but now the cyborg felt different. More human, yet less at the same time. And her aura was a twisting spiral of chaos as if two personalities were at war with itself. Perhaps it was from the damage she'd sustained, but whatever the cause, Hendrix was clearly in trouble, which meant they all were as well.

But what should they do?

She could sense that Hendrix and the cyborg had traveled a fair distance down the corridor, a safe enough distance that she could creep out of the shadows now. If she headed back to the Queen Phoenix, she could leave this place and escape. But she was no pilot and leaving Hendrix behind without the means to awaken his people from stasis wouldn't only doom him and his kind, it would doom her sister and Axel and everyone on Amasis. And everyone in the galaxy, for that matter.

She needed to keep going with the plan already in motion and awaken the shifters from stasis, and she needed to do it before any more trouble arrived. If Thalia had managed to track them to this ship, the Core wouldn't be far behind.

"Life." Phoenix pointed to the corridor adjacent to the one that Hendrix and the cyborg had disappeared through.

Caree looked down at him. His beaming smile

filled her heart with warmth. He was growing so fast. She'd had no idea what being a mother would be like, but this amazing new being who'd come from her body was the biggest gift she'd ever been given.

He wanted her to go down that corridor to find the shifters, but how would they respond when woken? She'd relied on Hendrix being with her when that happened. It was in his best interest to protect her and Phoenix, at least until he got what he wanted from them. But he was a great warrior on his own. Imagining what one hundred and fifty of his kind would be like without him there was unnerving. What if they turned against her as soon as they were awakened? Or worse still, what might they do to Phoenix? They fed on energy and would be hungry. He was just a baby, but he might make an appealing source of food to starving shapeshifters. It was what the aliens on Amasis had wanted him for—to feed the mind-eaters and save the Stardrives. How were the shifters really any different?

She moved down the corridor as quickly and silently as possible. Her arms were beginning to tire from carrying Phoenix everywhere. But even if he could walk on his own, she wouldn't have chanced it. She had loved him since she'd learned he was growing inside her, and she used every portion of her strength to keep them both safe.

The faint blue Stardrive glow from his body enabled her to step carefully through the corridor, but she hoped that as he grew older, he'd learn to control it. It was a liability at the moment, and she'd just barely managed to hide him deep enough in the shadows to avoid being seen by the cyborg earlier. She wouldn't bank on being able to do so if they ran into Thalia again. She could just barely sense the cyborg and Hendrix traveling in a parallel direction. So far, the paths were divergent in their destination as the one the cyborg had chosen was a more direct route to the engine room. But they could change course at any moment.

And why the frell had humans built these ships so big with endlessly long corridors between chambers? Spokes on a wheel to create a central gravitational nexus created by an incredibly slow spin. It made sense, maybe, now that she considered it, but it seemed to be taking forever to get to the stasis pod chamber, each step more unnerving than the last. While the layout was familiar, the silence wasn't. Instead of being empty, it was full of expectations. The sleepers on board were haunted with the need to be awakened. Did they know she was there? Could they sense her presence?

An unspoken feeling told her to take a left turn just ahead. She did so and stopped when she saw a closed double doorway a few feet away.

No handle could be seen, only a small panel that relied on an imprint to operate it. As she examined the panel, a holographic display came to life, illuminating the image of a single upright palm.

"How am I supposed to open that?" she muttered. She didn't have shifter DNA, and this door would be keyed to that for sure. This situation was one of many reasons why they needed Hendrix with them.

Phoenix's gaze met hers. '*Try,*' his thought spoke into her mind.

She wasn't sure what that would accomplish, but it wouldn't hurt to do as he suggested. She shrugged and placed her palm over the image.

A surge of energy passed through her, causing a pulse to arc through her palm and into the holographic array and her to jump back in surprise.

The door immediately unlocked and hissed open, allowing them entry to the chamber beyond.

Caree glanced at Phoenix and flexed her hand. Her palm tingled where the energy had exited. "You did that, didn't you? Amplified my energy with yours?"

He smiled and giggled quietly, clearly pleased with himself.

Caree shook her head. Her baby was full of surprises.

She stepped through the doorway into the darkened room. As the door closed behind her, several strips of ceiling lighting lit up one section at a time. For as far as she could see, the room contained clusters of cylindrical semi-transparent stasis pods, their contents obscured by a white mist inside each one.

She didn't try to work out how many of these compartments were in the room, but it was easily more than one hundred.

Over a hundred shifters, she thought and paused walking as the reality of being surrounded by so many hungry shifters settled in her mind. Was there another way to wake them? Perhaps she should head to the bridge and see if the Stardrive could be saved first. The energy from that dying orb would be more useful here as well as safer for her and Phoenix, but that was where Thalia and Hendrix had been headed. It was better to stay where she was and do what she could as quickly as possible.

"Friend," the baby said. He began to kick his legs and bounce up and down in her arms. His excitement about being near all the shifters was making it hard to hold him.

"You trust them?"

He let out a squeal and wriggled so much, she nearly lost her balance.

"Okay, okay!" She laughed as she walked forward into the large room and toward the nearest cylinders. They were arranged in groups of five and connected by one end like spokes on a wheel to a central column where controls were displayed. Caree walked between two of the cylinders and examined the controls. The display was filled with unfamiliar lettering, probably the original Earth language from the ship's inception. But she didn't need to read it to understand what the accompanying flashing red images meant. The power to keep the beings inside the cylinders in stasis was at a critical level. In fact, some of them in this cluster had already failed, the screens dark and unresponsive. If they didn't act fast, they would lose them all.

Caree sat Phoenix on the nearest semi-transparent cylinder.

He patted the smooth surface with his tiny hand and said, "Life."

The gas inside the cylinder swirled in an accelerated pattern as if responding to his presence. He smacked his palm against the surface, and a current of energy shot from his hand and arced over the pod to the control mechanism. There was a popping hiss of over-heated electrical conduits and the tang of ozone. Then the mist slowly dissipated from the capsule, and the naked body of a human male became observable through the container.

"Friend," Phoenix said again.

Caree nodded. She'd have to accept her son's

judgment, as she didn't possess the abilities to do so herself. She picked Phoenix up from the capsule as the gas completely disappeared. A palm-shaped holographic panel like the one that had operated the doorway into the room appeared on the central control console of the cluster.

"Let me guess," Caree said to Phoenix. "This activates the pod?"

"Life," the baby said.

"Okay." *Let's hope it's not our death,* she thought. She closed her eyes and let her son's energy course through her body as she raised her palm to the panel, certain there was no other way to proceed. They had to wake these shifters, but whether these aliens would be friend or foe was anyone's guess. She hoped between Phoenix and her, they could overpower any problems they might encounter.

6

"No... please don't, he's just a baby," Ellie pleaded with the large-eyed alien.

"The child is needed to feed the plague and restore energy to the Stardrive vines. One life for the good of the galaxy," the gray-skinned being said.

Caree lay nearby with her arms around her knees, sobbing uncontrollably as Phoenix was taken away by a group of aliens.

Ellie tapped Axel on the shoulder. "We need to do something."

He shook his head and looked her in the eye. "No, the Amasisans are right."

She took a step toward him and slapped him on the cheek, the contact causing her hand to sting while Axel's face turned sharply from the impact. "You're a dick, just like your brother."

The gray beings surrounded her, restrained her arms and legs, and carried her away. She screamed and tried to struggle, but their hold was strong despite their small stature.

"We can't afford to risk another outburst from you." The leader of the group pointed at Ellie. "We're taking you to a lab where the mind-eaters can feed from your brain without interference."

"What? No!" She kicked out with such force she managed to loosen the hold on her left foot. It connected with the bulbous head of one of the nearest aliens causing a satisfying grunt to come from the creature before her body was once again restrained.

"You're a feisty little bitch, and while we're not in the business of killing, we can sentence you to this type of punishment indefinitely."

"Axel! Henry! Shiznit!" she yelled.

But it didn't matter. They were all gone now, and she found herself carried through a dark tunnel. The only sound she could hear was the movement of the aliens' feet slapping against the gray mud, and the smell of rotten meat soon made its way to her nose. The urge to gag caught in her throat as the scent filled her nostrils and her stomach twisted.

"Many have perished here over the years, but we leave their bodies to be consumed by the worms and the lice that grow in the soil. All life is precious." The leader spoke close to her ear. "And even in death, the bodies that once had life serve a purpose."

She hated the sounds of the alien's voice. Devoid of emotion, it may as well have been talking about the components of a starship. The tunnel continued on and on, and the need to vomit increased with every turn they took in the path.

"Here we are," one of the other aliens said. Ellie was thrust into a cage and restrained by cuffs around her wrists, midsection, and ankles. The cage was tall enough for her to stand in, but it was quickly tipped until she was lying flat on her back.

The aliens stared down at her, a ring of black-eyed faces. Then she couldn't see anything but opaque white as a bright light was placed above her eyes, and something cold touched her temples.

"There's no escape," the alien whispered near her ear. Or maybe it was inside her head.

She blinked and tried to shut out the light.

To move.

To speak.

To think.

This isn't real.

This isn't real.

This isn't REAL.

But she wasn't sure anymore.

7

As the cover slid open and the remnants of the white mist dissipated, the human-shaped being lay still as death inside the stasis pod. It was impossible to tell that the being wasn't human. His mostly naked form was identical in proportion to any human she'd ever seen. Maybe a bit smaller in parts than Axel and definitely smaller in parts than Kendrick. But his pale-skin and dark-haired gruff appearance reminded her most of Hendrix.

She checked the readouts on the console. A green light blinked steadily. It appeared that the shifter was alive and was no longer in stasis. But it needed something more to be fully awakened. *Time maybe?* But they didn't have the liberty of time.

Phoenix reached toward the shifter with both arms outstretched. "Touch."

Caree nodded, struggling to maintain her grip on him as he wiggled. He was strong and getting stronger by the minute. She placed him on the shifter's chest, keeping a hand on his back more for her reassurance than his. Body contact was a way she'd used to channel healing energy with others, most recently with Axel when she'd been a conduit for the Stardrive that had saved him from death. But watching Phoenix attempting the same with this unknown shifter filled her with apprehension. Her child was so small and innocent. Defenseless.

The baby slapped his hand on the shifter's chest. A jolt of energy surged through Phoenix and arced like a blue streak into the prone being.

The shifter's eyes flashed open. Its chest heaved on a gasp. It grabbed at the baby and clutched the child by the arms.

Phoenix squealed, but Caree couldn't tell if it was from excitement or pain. Her heart raced as the being's intense hunger filled her. This creature wanted to feed. And the small child sitting on its chest was just what it needed. This was what she had feared—the shifters would harm her child while he tried to help them.

"No!" she shouted as she lifted Phoenix away from the shifter and braced for a fight while doing so. But the being let the baby go without trouble, its hands falling back down into the pod as if they suffered from increased gravity.

"Hungry." Phoenix kicked his legs, a pout puckering his lips. But instead of reaching for the shifter, he stuck his thumb in his mouth and clung to her.

Caree studied the shifter. Its eyes were closed, and it appeared weak. It needed food, but no frelling way was she going to let him feed off her baby again.

She looked over the console. There had to be a solution. The diagrams showed various controls, one of which monitored the bodily processes of the being inside the stasis pod.

She pressed a button that seemed most likely to indicate recovery processes. A panel opened on the console, and a slender drawer slid outward. It contained several pouches of liquid nourishment. She grasped one and held it outward to the shifter. It wasn't Stardrive energy, but maybe in this human form, human food was what the shifter needed during this part of the recovery period.

"Hungry," Phoenix repeated.

The shifter opened its eyes and looked at the baby, then at Caree and the pouch of nourishment she held in her hand. A flicker of recognition passed over its features. It slowly raised a hand, reaching for the pouch.

"I guess you do feed like a human right now," Caree said. She'd been so focused on what Hendrix had said about shifters needing Stardrive energy to survive, she had not considered the fact they would also need food that their assumed form required for nourishment. She opened the spigot on the pouch and passed the container to the shifter.

It grasped the tube and put it to its mouth, closed its eyes, and began to sip.

Caree smiled and looked at Phoenix. "Maybe this is going to be okay, after all."

Phoenix grinned and pointed to another capsule.

"Are you sure about this? We need to move quickly, but you don't have unlimited energy." Caree frowned. He replenished most of his energy from her and whatever nourishment he got from the nutritional bars she'd been supplementing her breast milk with. She was going to have to feed him soon, and herself too.

"Friend," Phoenix said. "Help."

Did he mean Hendrix or the shifters in stasis? It was hard to tell. Maybe all of them. But how many would they need to wake to solve the immediate problem of Thalia? And how long would it take for the shifters to recover from being in stasis for so long? What if Thalia found them before the shifters were recovered? The cyborg was strong, and Caree had seen what her stasis gun was capable of. She glanced at the first shifter they'd awakened, who was still sipping the nutritional fluid with its eyes closed. Thalia could easily kill all the shifters in this vulnerable state. Hopefully, it wouldn't take too long for the shifters to regain strength. And hopefully, Hendrix would keep Thalia occupied for a bit longer without getting himself killed in the process.

Caree nodded. “Let’s hurry.”

She assisted Phoenix to activate the capsule he pointed at and repeated the exact process he used to wake the first shifter. This one was a female, brown-skinned and dark-haired. As she gave the newly awakened being a nutritional pouch to consume, Phoenix glanced about the room.

“More.” His tiny brow was furrowed. The blue glow of his skin seemed diminished. She spared a moment and fed him quickly, her energy depleting as his increased. She nibbled a piece of nutritional bar as he fed, rocking him gently in her arms.

Movement made her glance to the side. The first shifter was now sitting upright in the pod, observing them while he finished the contents of the nutritional pouch.

She disengaged Phoenix from her breast and nodded at the shifter. “We’re with Hendrix. I don’t know what his name is in your language. Or even if he’s a he,” she added. Did fluid species have specified gender identities? Did it matter? She decided to keep going with what she knew. “He’s on the ship, but he’s in trouble. We all are. We need help.”

The being observed them silently, his expression devoid of anything except curiosity. She couldn’t read him beyond his ravenous hunger. Whatever shielding this ship had continued to affect her ability to sense things. Or maybe it was just her. Things had been different since she'd given birth to Phoenix. In some ways, her empathic ability seemed stronger, and in others, diminished.

"Friend," Phoenix said.

"Are you sure about that?" What if her son was wrong? For all his advanced abilities with perception, he was still a baby and innocent of deception.

Her trust in the situation was diminishing by the second, even as her frustration increased. It was taking too long to do what they needed and exposing them to too much risk. There had to be a better way to do this. Devoid of other options, she kept an eye on the first two shifters as Phoenix began to wake a third. The male's attention was now focused on the nearby pod where the second shifter was sitting upright. The two of them stared at each other in silence, their expressions blank of anything Caree could read to understand their intentions, except their need to eat. It wasn't a good feeling, being so unconnected, but there was nothing she could do about it. Did these beings communicate telepathically? Not a human trait, usually, but they continued to stare at each other as if words were passing between them.

"Figures…" the dark-skinned woman stated, breaking the silence. Her voice was soft, barely audible, and raspy with lack of use, "...That you would make it."

She raised herself from the pod, her nude appearance apparently not much of a concern to her comfort, and without another glance at anyone else, she headed slowly for the door. Each step was shaky, as if her coordination was impaired by muscles long unused.

The first shifter moved to follow, raising himself from the pod, and nearly collapsed from the effort. "Figures that you're still a bitch," he muttered. He limped slowly after the woman shifter, ignoring Caree and Phoenix as if they were invisible.

"Wait. Where are you going?" Caree called out to them. "It's not safe."

The woman turned toward her. "To find more food. We must eat. That blue thing is bitter." She gave a disgusted flip of her hand at the baby. Caree glanced at her son. The shifters didn't like how Phoenix's energy tasted? Well, that was a relief. "You are—"

"Bad," Phoenix said. He clutched at Caree so tightly he nearly knocked her off balance. She struggled to hold onto him and leaned back against the console between the two nearest pods.

"What? The shifters?" Her pulse pounded as the baby's thoughts raced through her mind even before the question escaped her mouth. *'Bad, bad, bad!'*

She slid down the console and onto the floor out of sight, holding him tight, not quite certain where the danger was coming from—the shifters, the cyborg—but knowing that they needed to keep hidden as best they could. Tucked behind the pods, she tried to steady her breathing, but while her view of the room and the awakened shifters was obscured, the sound of the doorway opening was loud and clear.

"Well, well, well, what do we have here? It looks like you have finally got me what I wanted." The cyborg's voice carried through the room a second before the sound of her stasis gun firing. "Thank you, handsome. I'll take two."

Hendrix surveyed the situation with a quick glance—the opened stasis pods, Caree and Phoenix nowhere in sight, and two of his kind awakened but clearly weak and still in human form. Not much use to him beyond a distraction, but a distraction was all he needed. Hendrix moved as soon as the cyborg's attention switched from him to the two shifters standing near the doorway.

He lurched sideways and grabbed Thalia's arms as she aimed the stasis blaster at the nearest shifter. The shot went wide, but with her cat-like reflexes, she spun out of his grasp and raised the gun at him.

He dodged and rolled backward. The electric-like bolt of energy that she fired flew above his head. His newly awakened brethren were retreating toward the safety of the stasis pods. Too weak to shift and unarmed, there was nothing else to do but hide.

Thalia swung her stasis gun from him to the others and fired at them. A single shot each was all it took to instantly paralyze them. They fell to the ground, mid-step. Thalia trained her gun at Hendrix and studied him with her brow raised.

The moment stretched while he waited for her to pull the trigger. "Why don't you kill me? You got what you wanted." The last of his people. In Rosamunde Cruz's control. He didn't want to see what would become of them.

Thalia bent low over him. A grin split her lips. "Oh, what kind of fun would that be, handsome?" She prodded his chest with the tip of her blaster.

Hendrix stared at her. What game was this that she was playing now? Her tone changed with that last retort. Playful. Familiar in cadence. Iris had called him handsome. But why would a cyborg want to impersonate a pirate? What kind of trap was this?

Thalia moved the tip of the blaster down his

midsection and rested it on his groin. Her gaze flicked to his. Teasing. Coy. Emotions a cyborg never should have unless her programming had been drastically altered. "Have you missed me?"

"Missed you?"

Her brows flicked. A pout pulled down her bottom lip. "After all the fun we had together." She stood up straight and pointed the gun at his head, her expression an impenetrable mask devoid of emotion once more. "He has forgotten you, sister."

Her lips twisted as she licked them. "We could have a lot of fun reminding him." She cocked her head. Her expression changed, turning cold.

"He does not even know who we are. He no longer serves any purpose."

The stasis blaster quivered in her hand as if she was struggling to keep it pointed at his head. Hendrix stared at it and the cyborg. What the frell is going on? Could a cyborg suffer a psychotic break? She appeared to be arguing with herself as if she was two different people.

"Do you not remember your promise to me?" she asked him, her voice sounding almost pleading.

He nodded, thinking fast. "Yes. I promised to kill you if I ever saw you again."

She laughed and shook her head. "That was what you promised her. To avenge me."

He stared at the shaking gun in her hand and then into her eyes. There was pain there—

indecision—as if begging him for recognition. He'd promised to kill Thalia for killing Iris. Was it possible part of her programming had been corrupted at that time? The cyborg had been shot in the head. What if her memory of killing the pirate had been transferred into her thinking she was the pirate? His pulse beat fast. Whatever had happened, this cyborg was dangerously unstable. One wrong word could end all their lives. "Who are you?" he whispered.

Her expression hardened, and the switch was instantaneous. One personality gone, and in its place the cold, expressionless cyborg. The stasis blaster in her hand stopped shaking. "We will not be forgotten. This conversation is at an end."

The sound of movement behind her drew both their attention. Caree stood with Phoenix in her arms no more than half a meter away. The baby had his hands outstretched toward the cyborg, a blue glow pulsing around them.

"Bad!" the baby shouted.

The blue glow shot from his hands, a bright ball of energy that impacted the cyborg with a flash. It traveled through her, knocking her to the ground. A portion exited through the stasis gun, adding its energy to the blast. The discharge sounded like thunder, echoing off the walls of the room. Or maybe that was what it sounded like as the energy seared through Hendrix's skull.

And then it sounded like silence as he slipped into nothingness.

8

"..." the portable comm unit buzzed, "..."

"Hendrix."

"Hendrix..."

"Hendrix... Hendrix... do you copy, Hendrix?" a male voice squawked over the comm unit.

Hendrix blinked and looked around as the white mist that clouded his thoughts like a heavy fog dissipated. He was somewhere familiar. A room. On a ship. But not the Millennial vessel he'd left the shifters on. He was up against a wall with guns trained at his head. *Oh, shit, this was a memory. But not just any memory. This was the time he'd become—*

"Officer Nigel Hendrix." The bigger of the two Core officers who had him pinned down was reading off Officer Hendrix's stats from a holographic scan. "Born in Boston, Massachusetts, Earth year 2965. Joined the Core in 2982, transferred to Covert Operations in 2984, and promoted to Intelligence Commander in 2987." He tilted the image and looked at Hendrix. "That's a pretty quick rise. I'm impressed."

Hands held in the air, Hendrix didn't reply. He darted a glance downward at his helmet, which lay on the cargo bay floor about a half meter from his feet. Despite the damage his headgear had sustained when it had been forcibly removed during the fight, his comm was apparently still working.

Just like it had happened in the past. How long had it been since he'd become Hendrix, the human ex-military mercenary? Five Earth solar cycles? Six? An eternity? He'd absorbed all the human's thoughts and feelings, his consciousness, everything that had made up his being, including his last actions before death. But the memory of that moment of transition seemed as crisp and real now as then.

In a fluid motion, Hendrix snatched his laser bolter from his holster and fired off a quick shot before the two Core bastards could completely disarm him.

The large-headed Travanian officer in front of Hendrix grabbed the weapon from him as the other Core grunt, a human, froze Hendrix against the wall with a blast of stasis webbing.

The Travanian's glance shifted between the

blackened remains of the comm and the mercenary. "Smart. Real smart." He leveled the blaster at Hendrix's gut and squeezed the trigger.

At point-blank range, the blast went clean through his protective body armor and left a searing thumb-sized hole in his flesh. Hendrix let out a hiss of pain and would've doubled over if he'd not been held up by the stasis webbing that covered his chest and pinned him in place.

"Did that hurt?" the human asked, leering at Hendrix through his half-visor. He turned to his comrade-in-stupidity and grinned. "It sounds like it hurt."

The Travanian punched Hendrix in the gut. "That's what you get for destroying evidence."

Hendrix breathed deeply, ignoring the wave of nausea and pain that seized him. The memory he was experiencing wasn't fresh or even his own. It was the thoughts and feelings of the dying officer, which he'd incorporated after shifting into his form. But the shock of being seared by a laser blast still hurt like a sonofabitch and was just as real to him as if he'd experienced it firsthand. All of this was. He sighed mentally. It wasn't the first time he'd been shot as a human or a shifter, and it wouldn't be the last.

The human patted Hendrix's cheek. "Just a taste of what's to come. Don't want you to die too quickly now, do we?" He smiled, showing a mouth full of discolored teeth and a waft of stank breath strong enough to knock over a mob of flying Braptors.

"Not until you tell us who the buyer is for the illegals you've been smuggling," the burly Travanian said. He smashed Hendrix's wound with the butt of his blaster.

"Fuck!" The mercenary squeezed his eyes shut and took a steadying breath. He should've stayed in bed with that hotter-than-hell pirate who liked to tease him with her claw-tipped glove. Instead, he'd taken this job for Tobias and his damned resistance cause. Just his luck his ship had been caught in a trap on his way out of Hell. At least he'd managed to destroy the navigation array and logs before being boarded by the Core dickheads. Too bad he'd not made it to the escape pod.

The human slapped Hendrix in the cheek, rousing him from the darkness his mind floated in. "You aren't a hero. You're a dead man. Tell us what we want to know, and we'll make it quick. Keep stalling, and we'll take you apart, piece by piece."

The Travanian aimed his blaster at Hendrix's right foot.

Despite his helpless situation, the mercenary kept a smug smile glued to his face. If this pair of idiots thought they had him beat, they were kidding themselves. "I'm not a smuggler," he said.

"Liar." The Travanian shot him in the foot. Hendrix screamed. When the blackness that engulfed his mind receded, he opened his eyes. The human was twirling a knife in front of his face, the sharp blade glinting in the bright light of the cargo ship's container area. The grunt's gaze was a bit too eager for Hendrix's liking, as if the guard enjoyed using the weapon and was looking for a reason to do so.

"Try again," the Core officer said, his breath a foul torture that made Hendrix want to pass out again. "Tell us who you're working for."

Hendrix barked a laugh. "If you don't know that already, you're a bigger idiot than I thought."

The Travanian punched him hard. A punch so well placed that Hendrix would've collapsed if the webbing had allowed him to. "You have some kind of fetish for pain?"

"I think he does." Officer Stank-breath touched the knife tip to Hendrix's gut wound and pressed it into the flesh.

The mercenary hissed. The pressure was enough to cause intense pain but not enough to cut deeply.

The grunt grinned and lifted the knife. He glanced between the fresh blood that oozed down the blade and Hendrix. "Take a good look at that. You'll be seeing a lot more of it very, very soon."

"We have reason to believe that you've been communicating with a group of pirates, known friendlies of the Collective, and that's who you intended to meet," the Travanian said.

Hendrix shook his head. “I work for the Trade Corporation.” It was true. He did. Sometimes. “I’m not transporting illegals.” Okay, well, maybe he was, but if these idiots hadn’t found the item he’d hidden in the escape pod by now, then it didn’t really matter what they thought was true.

The Travanian laughed, which, considering his species tended to avoid doing so, sounded like a death rattle instead of anything resembling happiness. “You’re a very bad liar.”

“You see,” Officer Stank-breath said, twirling the knife. “We already know all about you.” He pushed a sequence of holographic buttons on his wrist unit and pulled up an image of the mercenary along with his stats. “We know why you left, don’t we? You’re working for the Freedom Collective, smuggling illegals and doing their dirty work, which makes you a traitor and a dead man.” The grunt twirled the knife in front of his face.

“Mind pointing that thing somewhere else?” Hendrix asked.

The guard grinned. “Not at all. I like knives.”

“But not dental hygiene. Duly noted.”

The guard placed the knife tip against the corner of Hendrix’s lips, causing a slight sting and the immediate tang of blood. “I’m getting really tired of your mouth.”

“Leave off,” the Travanian ordered Stank-breath. “We still need him able to talk.” He focused on

Hendrix again. "If you think you've covered your tracks by destroying the comms and the logs, you're more pathetic than I thought." He spoke into his comm. "Officer Franklin, bring it in."

"Copy that, sir," a voice replied over the open comm connection.

Shit. Hendrix willed himself to remain calm as his blood shot through his veins. Immersed in the memory as he was, there was no division to where Hendrix-the-human ended and Hendrix-the-shifter began. Their pain, panic, confusion, thoughts were the same. But this part, if he could forget it, he would without question.

The cargo bay door opened, and a human officer walked into the room. The grunt carried a small container, holding it out before him as if it might bite him. He seemed nervous, shaking slightly as he stopped by the Travanian and glanced between the two Core grunts.

Hendrix grinned. Maybe he did have a shot here. It was probably the kid's first mission. The skinny shit was still being potty-trained.

"I have the illegal, sir." The newcomer handed the container to the Travanian and turned to leave the room.

"Officer Franklin, were you dismissed?" Stank-breath asked.

The young man stopped and darted a glance at his fellow officers. "Uh, no, sir. Sorry, sir."

"Then where the hell are you heading? Get your ass over here." Stank-breath pointed at a spot on the floor beside him, and Franklin hurried to obey.

Frelling shit. Hendrix sighed. The Core never changed. Assholes were always assholes, even to other assholes. "It's okay, kid. There just seems to be a bit of a misunderstanding here," Hendrix said, hoping to seem disarming and establish sympathy. Or at least buy himself time until he figured out what else to do. But thinking was becoming more difficult as if a haze dogged his thoughts. Maybe he was bleeding heavier from his wounds than he'd first thought. "Someone is setting me up. I've never seen that thing before."

"Really?" The Travanian turned the box in his hand. The blue glow shining from the inside of it lit his features with a wan paleness. "So, an illegal container of proto-energy just happened to stow away on your ship by itself?"

Hendrix's smile broadened. "Yeah." It wasn't proto-energy, but they could think what they wanted. Better they didn't realize it was a fragment of a Stardrive—the rarest substance in the galaxy—and worth far more to humanity than these idiots could ever imagine.

"Franklin, do you know what proto-energy is?" the Travanian asked, keeping his gaze and blaster trained on Hendrix.

The young officer studied the container and

shook his head. "No, sir."

"It's a prohibited substance is what it is," Stank-breath said. "And this asshole says it just happened to find a way onto his ship." The knife-wielding guard gripped the hilt of his weapon tighter.

"Hey, now. I've never seen that container before. I don't even know what it does."

The Travanian shrugged. "Franklin, I want you to use your blaster and shoot it."

"No!" Hendrix shouted as Franklin pointed his blaster at the container. "You'll blow this ship up, including all of us."

Franklin paused and glanced at the Travanian.

"Ah, so you're familiar with it then." The large-headed grunt grinned. "Who were you delivering it to? The pirates you've been in contact with or the Collective? We know both use it for powering weapons."

"I don't know what you're talking about."

The Travanian made a disapproving clicking sound. "Nigel Hendrix, you were observed in the company of Iris Crane, a female pirate and known smuggler connected with espionage against the Trade Corporation. If you tell us where she is, we might let you die quickly."

"Bullshit! What kind of garbage are you trying to make up here?"

"We're wasting our time," Stank-face said. "Let's just kill him and put his head on ice. Intelligence can get what they want from it."

"This is bull—"

Franklin fired the blaster twice, hitting the Travanian and the human in the head. At near point-blank range, the shots were deadly, and both officers slumped to the floor, unmoving.

Franklin caught the container in his hand as it fell from the dead Travanian's grasp. "Come on, Hendrix, we need to get out of here."

Hendrix stared at the grunt. Maybe it was the blood loss and his vision being off, but he could swear the grunt was flickering as if his form were becoming blurry and unstable.

"Why?" he asked as Franklin undid the stasis web that held Hendrix in place against the wall.

"I couldn't let those idiots live, could I?" Franklin's grin seemed to slide over his face.

Hendrix shook his head to clear it. There was something very wrong with him. "Do you work for the Collective?"

Franklin smiled. "No." He held the container in one hand and wrapped his free arm around Hendrix. As they took a step forward, Hendrix stumbled. His legs were like rubber and his body like lead.

Franklin looked at him, and a frown crossed his features. Hendrix was grateful it managed to stay where it should, unlike his smile. A sliding mouth was hard to watch.

"You're not going to make it," Franklin said. "I was too late, I'm sorry." Franklin's hand holding the container seemed translucent and more like a tentacle now.

"I think...." Hendrix coughed. "I think that knife... had something on it." *Poison. I've been poisoned.* His words were as slurred as his vision. *Well, hell. At least I match,* he thought, which was an odd thing to be grateful for when dying.

"If I can get you to an escape pod, I'll put you in stasis and find someone who can give you an anti-toxin."

"An anti-toxin? From the Core military? Ha-ha, you're adorable, kid. I'm dying. The best thing you can do is pass me the blaster, leave this party, and tell your superior officer that I shot these two after they stabbed me."

"I've got a better idea." Franklin increased his grip and pulled Hendrix along the ground.

"You're crazy, kid." Hendrix coughed again, leaving tiny flecks of bright red blood on his black glove. "Just leave me here."

Franklin smiled. "No, that doesn't work for me."

Hendrix frowned. "Why do you want to help me?" There was something very odd with this kid. He wasn't acting like a typical Core grunt at all. If he was a spy, then who for?

The young Core officer didn't reply as he shouldered Hendrix's weight and half-dragged him to the door. He opened the cargo bay exit and peered through. "It's clear. The rest of my squad are still on the bridge, trying to undo the damage you did."

"Do you even know where you're going, kid?" Hendrix asked. The corridor seemed to shimmer and shake just as much as Franklin. "This way." He pointed left, then let his arm fall back to his side. This being alive and keeping on moving idea seemed to take far more effort than it was worth. "You know these ships have more escape pods than they let on? It's a safety regulation, ever since—"

"Save your energy," Franklin said. "The one we want isn't far ahead."

They managed the short distance to the destination, and Franklin opened the door, which led to an antechamber where the escape pods were located. The grunt picked one and pulled on the handle, opening the oval-shaped craft, large enough for two humanoid beings to occupy.

Placing the container on the floor, he strapped Hendrix into the seating and pushed a few buttons on the controls. As he took the opposite chair, the pod's thrusters ignited. In seconds, they were away from the ship.

Hendrix watched as his cargo vessel, The Bounty, disappeared into the blackness. He'd loved that ship. It hadn't been the best, but it had served him well through some dark missions, much like his body had done during his life. "They'll just follow us when they realize I've escaped. You should've left me behind."

"No, they won't." Franklin smiled as he dug into his waist pouch and pulled out an oblong, palm-sized device, and damn if his mouth wasn't sliding all over his face again. "I left them a little surprise." He pushed a sequence on the remote detonator, and the window glowed orange with the distant flash of an explosion.

"Shit," Hendrix said. "Who the frell are you?"

Franklin stared at him. He touched the container of Stardrive material, and his body began to shimmer and blur. In a moment, Hendrix was staring at an exact replica of himself, down to minute detail. Everything was the same—hair, clothing, even the scar on his face.

"Wha-what's happening?" He tried to back away, but there was nowhere to back away to, confined in the pod, his body shaking from the exertion of just staying alive.

"Don't be frightened," the replica of himself said in his exact tone of voice. "I only mean to help."

"Damn," Hendrix closed his eyes. "Can't I even die without going Braptor-shit insane?"

"Your eyes aren't fooling you. I'm a shapeshifter."

"That's impossible. Shifters are extinct." And had he always sounded like a prick when he talked? No wonder he'd not had much luck in his life with the ladies.

"Not all of us."

Hendrix cracked his eyes open again. "What do you want from me?" It was hard to catch his breath.

"You're too far gone now for me to save, even if I put you in stasis." The shifter's eyes were filled with sadness. "This wasn't part of my plan, I'm sorry. But in this way, I can help you live."

"So, you think it's okay just to take over my body?" Hendrix ground his teeth together as a spasm of pain gripped him. "Fuck!" If life wasn't shit enough, did dying have to hurt? And fuck this shapeshifter stuff. Fuck it all to hell. He was probably dead already and hallucinating his last moments while his brain suffocated from lack of oxygen.

He coughed and glared at the copy of himself. "Just because you look like me doesn't mean you'll pass off as me."

"I've inherited all your memories and your genetic coding. Everything that makes you, you, is now me. I've never met Iris Crane, but you have, and I could tell you exactly what she looks like. And feels like." His brows lifted as if the memories were humorous. "You really had a thing for her."

Fucking shapeshifters. Hendrix hissed, his thinking was coming in gasps, just like his breath. There was blood—he could taste it but couldn't think why it was bad. He was cold. So cold. This wasn't how it was supposed to end. He had so much to do. And Tobias needed that spark of Stardrive energy to help him find more. It was important. So important.

He thought of Earth. Of the scorching hot sun and thin atmosphere that forced them all to live underground. But he remembered green grass and how it had felt to walk on it as a child. Of long days spent talking and trying to find a solution to the energy crisis. Of his days fighting for the Core and spying for the Collective. And Axel, who'd been like a little brother to him. What would happen to him if he didn't make it back? What would happen to them all?

He focused on the dark shape sitting across from him in the void. "There's a man…" Hendrix coughed again. "Hen… Ry… Ryan. You need to take… and Tobi… as. Take… spark… to…"

The dark shape placed a hand on Hendrix's shoulder. "I know. I will. I'm so sorry it ends like this."

Hendrix focused on breathing for the next moments. How long did dying take? This agony seemed to be stretching for an eternity. If the end were inevitable, he'd rather go out on his own terms. Where was his blaster? He couldn't lift his arms to find it. He focused on the dark shape leaning toward him.

"Kill. Mm… e." Hendrix struggled to form the words. Dying hurt far more than he ever thought it could. Far more than he thought he should still be able to feel. Weren't people supposed to become numb with the cold as the blood stopped pumping through them? "End… now. Pleasss." The pain was so bad he couldn't get the words to form. It was time to leave. He knew it in his bones.

He closed his eyes. The pause seemed to last forever. Then he felt the tip of a blaster touch his temple. The cold metal should've inspired fear. But now, at this moment, he felt relief.

"You're a brave man, Nigel Hendrix. I'll honor your memory."

"… nnn… owww."

"For the galaxy," the shifter said.

Fuck, Hendrix thought.

And then he thought nothing.

But the shifter who was now Hendrix thought many things. He couldn't stop thinking and could not stop remembering all the lives he'd lived, all the beings he'd been, and the forms he'd taken and identities he'd assumed. Franklin. Hendrix. So many more he'd lost count. Each were a part of him now. But Hendrix, Hendrix had been different. Becoming him had changed his life and given him the chance to keep his promise to save his people. To save everyone.

Remember your promise.

You need to help them, Hendrix.
Help them, Hendrix.
Wake up!

9

"Hendrix… wake up… Hendrix!" a soft female voice quietly hissed.

"Asshole!" a child shouted.

"Phoenix, no. That's not very nice."

Hendrix groaned as he blinked open his eyes. The room he was in appeared dim, the surface he was lying on hard as rock, and the child grinning down at him from its mother's cradling arms was just as ugly as the first time he'd seen it.

The shifter groaned louder as he slowly sat up, his body protesting every movement as if he'd spent the night emptying several bottles of Plovanian ale. "What the frell did you do to me?" He closed his eyes and rubbed the back of his aching neck with his palm.

"Um… well," Caree said. "We knocked out the cyborg with an energy blast, but it set off her stasis gun by accident and… shot you in the head. Sorry."

"Frell." That explained why he felt hung over. He opened his eyes and stared at her. "How long have I been out?"

Perched beside him on the table, Caree seemed to be having a hard time keeping his gaze, but the ugly baby squirming on her lap was grinning its disgusting toothless grin. She shrugged lightly. "I'm not sure. A while?"

"A while?" A while wasn't good. Not with the Core heading their way. "Where's Thalia?" He glanced around the dimly lit room, looking for the danger he knew must be present. The space was occupied by many figures speaking in low tones. Realizing who they were, he jerked upright, despite his aching head. "You woke the rest of them?"

"Some of them. We couldn't wake them all yet. We need more energy for that. But some are... beyond waking."

He studied the survivors of his kind in silence. The numbers hadn't been great to begin with. Of the one hundred and fifty souls who he'd protected by putting them into stasis, how many were left?

They were in the long-unused mess hall of the Millennial ship. The rows of tables, and the figures occupying them, were mostly discernable by the ambient glow from the food replication consoles. It was quiet, almost eerily so. He couldn't hear what anyone was saying, not in their energy patterns, not like he should be able to.

I waited too long. Left them too long. But he hadn't had any choice, had he?

"We put Thalia into a stasis pod. It seemed the best way to keep her contained. For now." She frowned. "I'm not sure how well stasis works on a cyborg."

Hendrix shook his head, then regretted it as the room continued to knock back and forth for a few seconds after he'd stopped his movement. "It doesn't matter. We need to wake the others and get out of here before the Core arrive. She's already told them where we are."

Caree gestured at the newly awakened shifters. "They need to eat before they can do anything else. Phoenix can't feed them all, and he needs to recharge too, so we figured, you know, human form... human food. It's not very tasty." She grimaced as she pushed a packet of nutritional supplements across the table toward him. "But maybe some food will help you?"

He glanced at the package, then tossed it back toward her on the table. "You might want to check on the expiration date. They haven't been touched since the original crew of humans was on board." That had to be over a thousand Earth years now. He ignored the supplements and glanced around the room. The shifters were moving as if they were ancients rather than in their prime. This wasn't good. Was it the effects of prolonged stasis? How much did they remember of life before assuming human form?

Caree gagged. She tossed the supplements aside as if the packet had bitten her. "Oh, frell! No wonder they tasted bad."

"Bad!" Phoenix screamed and then giggled.

Hendrix shook his head. "There's something seriously wrong with that kid."

Ignoring his comment, Caree slid a small box across the table toward Hendrix and said, "Do you think these food pods are expired too?" She anxiously glanced around the room at the shifters. "It's what most of them are eating."

"No Idea." Hendrix picked one up and held it between his thumb and forefinger. "Technically, they aren't even food." The round disk was a compressed collection of loosely structured amino acids that could take on any edible form when given instruction. Much like himself. Except for the edible part. "We didn't need to assume a human form until a few hours before our stasis sleep, so we never ate what humans ate. But these—"

Phoenix grabbed one out of the box and squealed as he tried to shove it in his mouth.

"No!" Caree yanked it out of her son's grasp before he could swallow it. "You have to cook it first, remember?" She smiled as her son pouted and looked as if he were about to cry as he stared longingly at the drool-covered pod in his mother's hand. "Yes, you can put the pod in the machine and press the buttons."

The child's expression brightened immediately.

Hendrix frowned. He didn't have time for baby tantrums. Or any tantrums. He had to get everyone awake and off the dead ship before the Core showed up, or it wouldn't matter anymore because they'd all be either caught or dead.

But moving took more effort than it should. In fact, everything was taking more effort than it should, especially thinking. He glanced around the room at the few of his kind who were present. The connection between Caree and her son seemed like the kind of telepathy he normally experienced with his own kind, but right now, for whatever reason, he wasn't. Was the ship's dampening field interfering with his ability? Had the stasis gun's blast to his head done more damage than he thought? He tried to shift form and couldn't. Like the rest of his kind, he needed more energy. Pod food would have to do because Caree's creepy baby was doing nothing except creeping him the frell out.

"Let's get Uncle Hendrix something to eat," Caree said as Phoenix pointed at the nearby food replicator and bounced about in his mother's arms.

"Uncle Hendrix?"

The shifter frowned as Caree lifted the baby close to the device. The baby threw the pod into the opening of the machine and smacked several buttons while Caree shut the cover on top of it. Phoenix squealed with excitement as the inside of the machine lit up, revealing the tiny food pod on the bottom surface. After a couple of seconds, a steadily increasing whine emitted from the ancient device, reminding Hendrix of an over-stressed motor. That couldn't be good.

He gave Caree a sharp glance as the whine increased and filled the room. "What the frell did that kid do?"

As the whine became ear-splitting, so did Hendrix's alarm, along with his certainty that things weren't going to end well in about ten seconds. The others stared at the replicator, seeming frozen in shock.

"It's gonna blow!" Hendrix shouted. He shoved Caree away from the replicator and dived down to the safety of the other side of the table. As he clenched his eyes shut expecting the worst, the whining ended as abruptly as it had begun.

No explosion.

No explosion?

Hendrix peeked out from behind the table. Caree and Phoenix stared back at him from where they had landed when he'd shoved them, studying him as if he'd lost his mind.

One of the nearby shifters who identified in the form of a female human, had risen from her seat and walked toward the machine. She opened the hatch on the food replicator and retrieved the tray of food that the pod had become. "Oh no." She glanced at Hendrix with a raised brow. "Be careful of the killer meat and potatoes."

The room rumbled with laughter.

Hendrix slowly got to his feet. He'd seen food replicators in action before, of course, but not one like this ancient one. He stared at the steaming food tray, which was packed full of meat cubes and perfectly spherical potatoes. There was enough food on the plate to feed ten humans.

"Are you not impressed, Hendrix?" the female asked. Placing the tray on his table, she grinned. "Grub's up, as humans say."

"Hey, Gothani. Are these potatoes made from organically grown amino acids?" one of the shifters asked as he walked over to sit at Hendrix's table.

"Are you serious?" Hendrix gave him a good once-over. He was beginning to sense their identities now. Zodial. This one was Zodial. They were each wearing flight suits with name tags sewn on the shoulder. Relics from long-dead former occupants as old as the ship were preserved as if new and brought to life again by the shifters.

"I'm a vegan and don't do carbs," another male shifter, Krystar, said, joining the others at Hendrix's table. He looked at the tray and frowned. "Isn't there anything else available?"

"For fuck's sake!" Hendrix yelled. "Do you lot not

understand the situation we're in?" What the frell had happened to them all during stasis? Had their minds become soft? Had he left them too long?

Gothani rolled her eyes. "Looks like somebody's got a case of the grouchies." She grabbed a plate of food off the tray and made a tsk-tsk sound as she shook her head. "Good thing you weren't left to rot in a stasis chamber for hundreds of years. You might not have survived." Without waiting for a reply, she headed toward another table and sat down.

Hendrix leaned back in his chair and studied the shifters. At Gothani's accusatory words, they had all stopped eating and were watching him instead. He glanced at each in turn. "I never abandoned you. I've been looking for a way to save us all, just like you chose me to."

"Easy words," the male shifter across the table from him said.

"Really? You've no idea what I've been through. If I'd wanted to abandon you, you'd be dead." He glanced at each of them. "Yet here we are, sitting around like we have all the time in the world, eating this shit..." he pushed the tray away from him, "... instead of getting the hell out of here before the entire Core fleet shows up."

"The who?" Krystar asked.

"You were supposed to bring a new Stardrive to fix things," Gothani said. She seemed to have taken up the cause of challenging him. "You were supposed to revive us all with it. But there are less than ten of us awake. And I'm not sensing a new Stardrive, just that… thing." She pointed at Phoenix. "What is it anyway? Some kind of biological hybrid? Well, we can't survive on it, can we? Its energy tastes like Borb vomit." She gestured at the expansive room. "Where's the new Stardrive, oh savior of the Memini race?"

Hendrix sighed. "I brought one with me, but it expired along the way."

"What? It just up and died before you could get here?" Gothani's lips formed a thin line. "What kind of crap are you trying to feed us?"

"Grade A crap, apparently," Krystar commented. "Stardrives don't just die."

"You're right. They don't. Not unless they're severely drained or damaged. I found a whole planet of them, enough to last us a hundred lifetimes and more if we take care of them. But it's infested with mind-eaters. The parasites have been feeding off them, weakening the stock. And the Amasisans have failed in their job as caretakers. We need to hurry if we want to save any of them."

"It's true." Caree's voice seemed quiet in the large space. She held Phoenix close to the replicator as he placed another food pod into the machine. "Yes, Phoenix, this is fun," the Endarian said in an exaggerated sing-song voice. She glanced around at the shifters, capturing their attention. "Hendrix is telling you the truth. We did have a Stardrive when we left Amasis to come here, but it didn't survive the trip. So, my child and I used our energy to wake who we could."

Krystar jerked his thumb in Caree's direction as he focused on Hendrix. "Who the frell are they exactly?"

"The female is a half-human, half-Endarian empath. The other is her mutant offspring, who's part-Stardrive."

A murmur rippled through the shifters.

"Part Stardrive?" Gothani rose from her chair as she studied Caree and Phoenix but didn't move toward them. She turned to Hendrix instead, her expression a mix of disbelief and apprehension. "How is that even possible?"

Hendrix shrugged. He'd been asking himself that since the child's conception. "The universe is one big frelled-up mystery?" But none of them could deny the reality that Phoenix existed, or that without his help, none of the shifters in the room would've been awakened. He nodded toward Caree and Phoenix. "But we owe a debt to these two, and it's a debt we need to repay."

"Yeah." Krystar eyed the Endarian and her baby suspiciously. "Why do I get the feeling I should've stayed in stasis."

Hendrix frowned. "Listen. I don't have time to

explain everything. You're just going to have to trust me. There's an entire fleet of the Core's finest on its way here. We need to wake the others and get off this ship before they do, or we're all going to be worse than dead." There was no way they could defend themselves or even shift forms until they got more energy, preferably from a Stardrive.

"You keep mentioning this Core? Who is the Core?"

"Two hundred and fifty years ago, they were called The Order. You know, the genocidal maniacs who hunted our kind like Braptors in a Goober cave? You remember them, right? The reason we had to hide in this broken hunk of human shit to avoid being exterminated? Well, thanks to that cyborg bitch you put in stasis, they've found us. So... *we need to leave. NOW!"*

The room became still for a moment as his words penetrated the cryo sleep-addled minds of the shifters.

Gothani visibly paled. "Shit."

"We should've dumped that cyborg bitch out an airlock," Krystar said.

"Wouldn't have mattered. The Core was most likely notified as soon as she got here."

"But how did she get here?"

"Hendrix was tracked, weren't you, Hendrix? How careless can you get?" Her glare carried the full force of her anger. "You should've left us all in stasis. You've killed us anyway."

"Let's just focus on getting out of here, not waste time fighting about who to blame."

"How?" shouted Gothani. "How the hell are we supposed to wake the others and get out of here without a Stardrive? This ship is dead. And so are we."

"No." Caree shook her head. "This ship isn't dead. There's a Stardrive here. It's very weak, but it still has power."

"Not enough to fire the engines and escape before the Core get here."

"True," Hendrix agreed. "But it might be enough to wake the others. I have a ship. It's small, but if everyone shifts to an amoebic form, we can all leave. But we need to act *now*."

"This better work," Gothani said. "Or I'll personally make sure the Core dissects you first."

It took more time than Hendrix liked to re-route what was left of the Stardrive's failing energy from powering the once-majestic ship to powering the stasis chamber and awaken the remaining shifters. And then even more precious time and the last of the Stardrive's life to revitalize the shifters and change most of them, except for two who were needed to assist with carrying the others to amoebic form for transport.

"What about the cyborg?" Gothani asked.

Hendrix shined his wrist-light onto the opened stasis pod before him and stared at the figure of Thalia, lying within. Once the Stardrive energy had been depleted, the ship had become dark except for emergency systems. It would get cold quickly, and oxygen would run out within the next hour or two once any remaining energy stored in the containment systems was depleted. Without the stasis pod being powered, the cyborg would awaken soon. "We take her with us."

"Why not leave her for the Core?" Krystar asked as he grasped one handle of the cargo container that held the shifters, and Gothani grasped the other handle. "Or chuck her out the airlock," she added with a grunt as they lifted the container between them.

"She may prove useful as a hostage." She was beginning to stir. He shot her with the stasis gun that she loved to use on him so much and lifted her limp body into his arms. It wouldn't work for long to restrain her. They would have to figure out a more permanent solution to keeping her under control. But he wasn't going to let Rosamunde Cruz's favorite pet slip through his fingers when so much was at stake and leverage would prove useful. He nodded at the others. “Let’s go.”

Phoenix was a dim blue glow, carried by Caree, leading the way through the darkened hallways. The shifters followed behind, carrying the container holding their brethren. The compact size of the shifters made for easy transport, but their weight was an issue, even for the anti-gravity lifters attached to the container.

Despite the uncertain lighting, Gothani’s grimace was visible as she and Krystar struggled to move quickly with the box. “Humans are weak as well as stupid,” she said, her voice sounding strained. “Making foolish ships like this with endless hallways. We should’ve changed into something more practical.”

“No time or energy,” Hendrix reminded them. “We can alter our forms when we get to Amasis, where there are plenty of Stardrives.”

“Guarded by mind-eaters,” Krystar said.

“Yes,” Hendrix agreed. “But we’ve dealt with them before.” He decided less was more with this conversation. They would find out what it was like on Amasis when they got there and how the mind-eaters would affect them or not, depending on which form they chose to fight them in.

They continued down the maze of long hallways taking small breaks when needed. The sense of urgency that had been plaguing him since they arrived at the Millennial ship seemed stronger than ever. It didn't help that he knew exactly what would happen when the Core got there if they didn't leave first. His run-ins with Rosamunde Cruz had never proven anything but dangerous. As they reached the airlock where the Queen Phoenix was docked, Hendrix paused. Gothani and Krystar placed the container onto the floor, and Caree had stopped in the middle of the airlock chamber in line with the door. She turned to Hendrix, the blue glow from Phoenix highlighting the shadows of her face and giving her a concerned expression. The baby was fussing and unhappy.

"Something's wrong," Caree said.

Hendrix nodded. He felt it too. He'd been on edge since they boarded the Millennial ship. The feeling had increased when Thalia had shown up. He gave the cyborg another blast from the stasis gun before she started waking again and placed her against the cargo container beside Gothani and Krystar.

The control for the inner airlock door was blinking with a red light.

"I'm not sure we should open that," Caree said.

"No choice. We're running out of time. We need to get off this ship." Hendrix moved toward the door, but as he did so, his sense of apprehension increased. Whatever Caree was picking up on was bothering him too. Was the Core already here, waiting on the other side to capture them? The exterior viewscreen was disabled, like most other systems on the ship.

Keeping the stasis blaster at the ready, he pushed the button to open the airlock. The inner door slid open with a hiss. A red light flashed in warning, illuminating the airlock chamber where the outer door should've been but wasn't. Instead, the only thing separating them from the dark void of space was the emergency forcefield that flickered and rippled in crimson waves.

"Shit," Hendrix shouted. He quickly hit the close door button, which hissed into place, further protecting them before the force field failed.

Gone, it was gone.

The entire docking area.

The Queen Phoenix.

All destroyed in what he could only assume had been a blast that had left the airlock irreparably damaged, the ship in pieces, and all of them stranded aboard the Millennial ship unless they could find another way off.

"Oh, frell," Caree whispered, her voice carrying loudly in the silence that filled the room.

Hendrix turned and stared at the others. "What the hell happened?"

"That was our way off?" Gothani asked.

"That *was* our way off," Krystar corrected.

"That's it, we're frelled," Gothani said. She cupped her head in her hands and started pacing back and forth beside the cargo container. "We're completely freaking frelled. There's no way to get off. There's no ship to escape in, and if we don't die from lack of oxygen first, the Core is gonna come and capture us. Great escape plan, Hendrix!"

Hendrix ignored her. He walked to where the cyborg was propped against the container and stared down at Thalia. "What did you do?" His voice was tense with the rage that filled him. The desire to use the cyborg as leverage was quickly changing to the desire to just rip her to pieces and eject her into space.

As if hearing his words, Thalia started to stir. She looked up at him, and a deep rumbling laugh issued from her throat. "Do you not like my surprise?"

Hendrix shot the cyborg again and again, freezing her twisted smile in place. The urge to keep going and end it burned through his fingers as he squeezed the trigger on the stasis gun a third time. He shook with the effort to restrain the impulse to kill her. As much as he wanted to end the bitch, they would need her more than ever as a bargaining chip when the Core arrived.

"Wait." Caree gently touched his gun arm with her hand. "She came in a ship. It must still be here. A vessel this big must have more than one docking port, right?"

"Blue girl has got a point," Krystar said. "We can take the cyborg bitch's ship instead."

Hendrix nodded. "Unless she disabled that one

as well." He slung the blaster over one shoulder and the cyborg over his other. Gothani and Krystar picked up the container between them.

Gothani glanced at Caree. "Which way?"

The empath looked at the baby she was carrying in her arms. They seemed to share a conversation without speaking, and then Caree nodded. "Phoenix says it's not far."

"Let's hurry then," Hendrix said.

Phoenix kicked his legs and seemed excited to be on the move again as he led them back down the hall and then a side corridor to a hopefully undamaged docking point.

The glow dimly lit this one from the nebula outside the ship, which was viewable through a window on the far side of the chamber, right angle to the airlock entry. This chamber was larger than the other, with access for dual ships to dock.

Hendrix placed Thalia against the wall and quickly opened the inner door of the nearest airlock docking point. It hissed open and revealed the closed outer door with a view of the ship docked on the other side.

"Frell," Hendrix muttered. The cyborg's vessel was a single-seat personal shuttle with limited space for one, let alone the rest of them. "It's too small for everyone."

"Well, what do we do now, fearless leader?" Gothani snapped, looking at Hendrix.

"Someone could leave and go get a bigger ship," Krystar stated.

Hendrix shook his head. "Not enough time."

"Well, we need to do something," Gothani said. "Because there's another ship coming in hot." She pointed at the wall where a proximity sensor had begun blinking.

"Shit." Hendrix hissed. "That's got to be the Core. Everyone, get into defensive positions. We're going to have to fight our way out and take their ship if we can."

Phoenix kicked his legs and squealed as if excited by the idea.

They formed a circle around the opposite docking point's inner airlock door. Krystar and Gothani were at the sides, and Hendrix taking point position. Caree ducked down behind the cargo container with Phoenix and peered over the top. They had the stasis blaster, his bolt rifle, and whatever energy blast Phoenix could conjure to immobilize the troops that came through the door. They could win this, couldn't they? They had to.

The ship drew nearer, its sleek design briefly visible through the airlock window as it flew into docking position, but without the computer to identify it, it was impossible to determine its size or class. If they were lucky, it was one of the Core's small transport carriers with a limited squad on board, but if they were unlucky, it was one of their armored personnel carriers filled with multiple squads of troops.

"Oh," Caree said. "I don't think that's the Core."

Hendrix glanced at her. She was getting to her feet and facing the door, a puzzled look on her face. Phoenix was kicking and clapping his hands.

"Well, who is it? Friend or foe?" Hendrix snapped at her.

"I guess that depends on why they're here," she said with a grin.

Frell it all. He didn't have time for bullshit. Their lives and the future of his entire species were at stake. He kept his blaster trained on the door as the airlock began to open.

Blake Bronson appeared in the opening instead of a Core trooper, his long dark coat swinging in the breeze as the air pressure within the air lock normalized.

"Heard you guys needed a ride," the captain of the Queen Bohemia said. He ducked a second later as a blast from Gothani's stasis gun narrowly missed his head and wiped the shit-eating grin from his face.

10

Rosamunde Cruz sat in her private office on board the Rose Thorne, drumming her fingers against the arm of her chair.

The ring of faces staring at her through the holographic emitter varied in appearance as much as species, but each shared the same reserved expression, and it was completely unacceptable. As representative members of the Galactic Trade Corporation, they each had the right to their opinions about galactic interests. However, to question her actions concerning Tobias Cruz's handling and death was beyond insulting.

She kept her tone measured as she addressed the assembled members. "As I have already stated, I abided by the standard rules of conduct regarding the withholding and questioning of suspected criminals laid out in Treaty 1138-B, subsection C. No impropriety occurred."

One of the members, Glass of Terra Prime, a small M-class world colonized by Earth, moved to speak, addressing her. "Prime Member, Cruz. Tobias Cruz was terminated without due process. He wasn't given the right to a fair trial. As a result, several outlying worlds have expressed reservation with joining our trade community as they fear how they'll be treated should any disagreement occur. Your reckless actions have cost us access to resources on at least three systems."

That claim caused a ripple of discontent, noises, and gestures of concern amongst the holographic representatives.

Rose stared at Glass. A bold move to try to accuse her in this way, considering his name had been associated with Tobias. Nothing to implicate him in any direct misdemeanors, but enough to generate suspicion. Perhaps it was time to investigate him more closely despite his strong standing in the trade community. Rose let the assembled members murmur for a moment. As soon as the fuss subsided, she addressed her accuser directly.

"Prime Member Glass, Tobias was a suspected key member of a known terrorist organization and posed an immediate threat, as I'm sure you're aware." She kept her gaze on him and let the words hang for a moment, heavy with implication. "If kept indefinitely for questioning, his incarceration would have generated sympathy for his cause. To release him would've sent a message that terrorist activity would be tolerated. An example needed to be made. Any prospective member who has chosen not to join us as a result would have caused issues anyway. I did you a favor."

The murmur started again, this time with nods and shrugs. If nothing else, the assembled were enjoying the show. The chance to exploit a perceived weakness was always a source of excitement.

"And what of the information learned during interrogation?" Chairman HO G287, a gaseous being elected to lead the assembly, asked through the use of a mechanical exoskeleton suit. "You indicated the inquisition of Tobias would provide key contacts that would result in the end of the Collective. We've yet to see any such information."

Rose tapped the arm of her chair with her fingers. Here, of course, was the real issue. Not Tobias's death but what his mind had contained. "I have shared with the assembly what has been proven accurate." She let her gaze settle on Glass once again. "And I continue to investigate leads."

"Be certain that you continue to do so," Chairman HO G287 said. "We've placed our trust in you in this matter, given that it's primarily under Earth's jurisdiction. However, if the outlying worlds will not join us to share their resources due to their lack of trust over your handling of Tobias Cruz, perhaps Earth can assist the galactic community in a greater manner to make up for any losses. We'll convene again in one-quarter solar cycle."

He moved to close the meeting, leaving Rose with nothing left to say except the usual, "Thank you, Chairman."

The holographic assembly disappeared as the connection ended.

She leaned away from the desk-mounted comm unit and gazed at the dark, comforting void of space through her skylight window.

How ironic that Tobias could still be a problem even dead. No, not ironic, but soul-burning, mind-searingly infuriating. If she could kill him a thousand times over, it would never be enough to make up for the trouble he'd caused by existing.

His scrambled brain had proven a treasure trove of information, all of which was of indeterminate value due to its questionable accuracy. A good portion of the access codes and locations of Collective strongholds had led to more dead ends than solutions, including anything that might directly implicate Glass, which had been perhaps the greatest disappointment. She'd been following Glass's movements for some time, waiting for the right moment to strike, certain he was key to the Freedom Collective as much as, if not more than,

Tobias. She'd wanted that victory to be now, delivered to her by Tobias, but instead, she was left with the unnerving feeling she was missing something critical.

The question of why slithered in Rose's mind, disturbing the peace the dark void provided.

Was it her fault Tobias's brain had proven less resilient during questioning than she'd thought? Torture was torture. Surely, the Galactic Trade Corporation understood that at times it might create less-than-desirable results. Sacrifices needed to be made to win this war and keep control of their assets. But to blame her for bungling the extraction of information? That was uncalled for. She was no screw-up, and yet it appeared that rumor had spread within the ranks that she was on the out with the corporation.

And it was all because her ex-husband was just what she'd always thought he was—a useless waste of skin, whose incompetence clung to her like an unpleasant stench.

Well, she'd worked too long and hard to establish her place in the galaxy to let him win by ruining it. Reputations could be salvaged, and when she was through with the Collective, they would regret ever doubting her. All she needed to do was gain the upper hand.

Rose called up a Core fleet commander on her holographic console. This woman had an appropriately bland expression, but there was a distinct tightness to the set of her lips.

"How soon will your fleet arrive at Amasis, Commander Randall?

"Our ETA is two Earth cycles. Once we've arrived, I'll inform you."

"I want you to set up a perimeter around the planet. Nothing is to get in or out without permission."

"As you wish, ma'am." The commander's gaze flicked away from hers as she disconnected the connection.

Rose stared at the empty holographic projector for a long second. There had been a subtle sneer in the way the commander of the Rehnquist had said ma'am, a behavior that had become increasingly familiar to Rose in her interactions with certain Trade Corporation personnel since she'd disposed of Tobias.

If it was true that Amasis was the home world of the legendary Visitors and it was the birthplace of Stardrive technology, then she needed to take control of it immediately as well as Caree and whatever mutant progeny the Endarian hybrid was carrying. The idea that the child could be part Stardrive seemed more likely a fallacy concocted by Tobias's fractured mind, but grains of truth were peppered within the mush his brain had become before he died, and if Caree had traveled to Amasis to have the child, Rose needed to find out why and gain control of the situation. Energy was the most valuable resource in the galaxy, and to have an unlimited supply was the key to all her plans. However, to achieve them, she needed to maintain complete loyalty within her Core officers.

She keyed a sequence into the holographic projector. This time a different officer aboard the Rehnquist appeared.

"Captain Ortega."

"Yes, ma'am." There was no wavering in this one's gaze or disrespect in his tone. Rose smiled.

"I have good news. It's time for Commander Randall to take an extended leave of absence. She may resist this idea, being so committed to her role of leadership, but you're to ensure that she, and any of her followers who find this sudden leave objectionable, receive a proper send-off by ejecting them out the airlock. Is that clear, Captain?"

"Yes, ma'am."

"Thank you, Captain. Your dedication will be generously rewarded." Rose keyed a code into her wrist comm and transferred half the pre-arranged credits into the captain's account.

His eyes brightened almost imperceptibly as his wrist comm pinged receipt of the funds.

Rose nodded. "You'll receive double my thanks when you've reported completion of this task."

"Thank you, ma'am." The Core officer nodded in

return, a quick bow of the head indicating he knew his worth and appreciated hers.

"And, Captain? You're Commander of the Rehnquist and its fleet now."

"Yes, ma'am. Thank you, ma'am."

Rose let the smile pulling at her lips unfurl. People needed to be reminded who was in charge and an example made of those who had forgotten. She had no illusion that obedience had anything to do with loyalty, as it was as easily sold as it was bought.

Ortega would go far as long as he continued to do what she wanted. And if not, well, there were always others who understood their place in her business.

Her wrist comm chirped and Gervais, her cyborg assistant while Thalia was away, announced, "My apologies, ma'am, however, a priority transmission has arrived from the Pelukan system that I have enhanced for you to observe. There is a great deal of interference."

The holo emitter flickered to life once again, this time displaying the captain of a different fleet of Core fighters. The image flickered and hissed with static but was clear enough to be understood.

"Ma'am." The captain gave a curt nod upon seeing her. "We've reached the coordinates within the nebula in pursuit of Thalia as directed. We have found a large ship matching the description of a

Millennial vessel. No life signs detected. However, a great deal of gamma radiation prevents us from using our navigational scanners with complete accuracy. Two smaller vessels appear to be docked on the—" the captain cut off as an officer interrupted.

"Sir, one of the smaller vessels is attempting to disembark."

Rose leaned forward in her chair. "Launch fighters and immediately pursue, Captain Pu-tau, but don't destroy. I want whoever they are to be caught and held for questioning."

"Yes, ma'am."

The transmission ended in a hiss of static. Rose pursed her lips and tapped them with her finger. Thalia had yet to report in, and it was possible that she was unable to do so for any number of reasons, but if the cyborg had left Amasis and entered the Pelukan system to rendezvous with the vessel, there must be a reason.

An ancient Millennial ship in an uninhabitable nebula?

"Gervais," she called into her wrist comm.

"Ma'am?"

"Have the captain send a team to investigate the Millennial vessel as well. I want to know what's on that ship and why it's there."

11

Caree clutched Phoenix tightly in her arms as the Bohemia accelerated away from the Millennial ship pursued by a squad of Core fighters, which had arrived shortly after Blake Bronson and the Bohemia. Hendrix, who was strapped into the seat beside her, watched Bronson intently, his aura dark and swirling with questions. He didn't trust this situation, not that he trusted anyone. He hadn't wanted to place the safety of his entire species in Bronson's hands, but the timely arrival of the Bohemia and its crew had allowed them to escape certain death or at least certain capture.

For the moment.

Maybe.

The ship banked sharply.

"Cutting it close, cutting it close..." Blake Bronson said, his voice raising with each iteration.

"Two more Core fighters are approaching from

the starboard, Captain," the cyborg navigator, T-183 said.

"Where the hell is the damned tesseract?" Bronson shouted.

"Forming directly ahead in eight space klicks," the Rhinernan co-navigator announced.

The Bohemia looked just like any other Queen-class vessel Caree had been on, except this one had a navigational array that was unlike anything she'd ever seen or could make sense of. But as always, Remler, the Rhinernan, and T-183, who co-manned the station, seemed to have little trouble understanding what the interactive holographic displays were telling them.

"The lead Core vessel has launched a shuttle. Trajectory indicates it will dock with the Millennial vessel in three-point five space klicks," T-183 said.

"They're going after the Millennial ship too?" Bubbles, the co-pilot, asked Bronson. "Who'd want that piece of space junk?"

"Anyone who thought there might be something interesting left on it," Thalia said. She was restrained against the wall where she'd been placed on a seat during the quick boarding, staring at Hendrix. Apparently, the last stasis blast she'd been given had worn off.

The mercenary raised the stasis gun and shot Thalia in the head again, silencing her.

Hendrix shared a quick glance with Bronson.

"Not all my people were able to be revived. Some had ceased existence. We left the bodies behind in the stasis chambers." The mercenary looked at the viewscreen, which showed the shuttle approaching the Millennial ship even as the Bohemia sped away, dodging the fighters tailing them. "I was focused on getting everyone off."

Bronson nodded. "But if Rosamunde Cruz gets her hands on those bodies, things will definitely go pear-shaped in the galaxy." He banked the ship into a vertical loop so tight that Caree pulled Phoenix even tighter to her, making the baby giggle. "We'll swing round and blast them to pieces before they can dock. Marsais? Take the gunner controls."

The cat-like Plovanian moved from her chair next to Hendrix to do as ordered.

"No, wait." Hendrix stopped her with his words. "I have a better idea." He pulled out the controls for the subspace pocket he'd hidden the Millennial vessel in for over two centuries. "Let them dock."

The smile that twisted his lips was filled with the grim memory of all the years of being hunted like rats as he'd once said to Caree.

Bronson dodged the fighters who continued to hail them, requesting they be escorted to the lead Core vessel for questioning. One fired a laser bolt at them, a warning shot meant to get them to obey.

Bubbles rolled her eyes. "Bullies. Always with the pew, pew, pew."

"Right!" Marsais said, taking her seat at the gunner station. "How are we supposed to surrender if we're dead?" She fired a laser blast back at the Core fighter, causing it to veer away or be hit.

"Just a bit closer." Hendrix watched the shuttle close in on the Millennial vessel for docking. "Just a bit more...." He keyed a sequence into the device.

The Millennial vessel appeared to waver on the viewscreen, a shudder Caree felt deep within her as whatever mechanism created the subspace pocket disrupted the normal void of space they were in. Then the screen lit up with a flash so bright she had to look away and shield Phoenix. The baby squealed and began to cry. She held him tight, soothing him with pats and reassuring words as the bright glow dimmed, revealing that the Millennial ship, as well as any ships caught in the blast, were reduced to little more than burning chunks of debris that were now hurtling toward the Bohemia.

"I thought you were going to strand them in subspace, not blow us all up!" Bronson shouted as the debris field expanded, threatening to overtake them. "Remler, get us out of here!"

"Amasis tesseract in three... two... one..." the Rhinernan navigator called out. A glowing vortex appeared before them as the main viewscreen switched views from aft to forward. The vortex lasted for a split second before they flew into it.

Then the viewscreen went blank as the fragmented Core vessels and the nebula seemed to disappear, replaced by nothingness.

Caree patted Phoenix as she looked around the Bohemia. They weren't dead or captured. They were somewhere within a tesseract. Whatever that was.

Phoenix let out a delighted squeal.

Bronson grinned as he turned to face the crew. "Exactly, new little buddy," he said, focusing on the baby. "That… is how we do it."

"And you did what exactly?" Hendrix asked. "I'm pretty sure it was me that blew the ships up."

"Well, we did happen to come along at just the right moment and save your ass. I'm pretty sure you were stranded." He looked at Bubbles. "They *were* stranded, right?"

She rolled her eyes. "Yes, there were stranded. Stop being dramatic and begging for compliments."

Bronson's grin widened as he studied Hendrix. "See? Stranded. Which means we saved your ass."

"You still haven't explained how you found us." Hendrix crossed his arms and looked at Bronson, unimpressed.

Bronson unstrapped his seat restraints and rose. "Let's just say this ship always ends up exactly where it needs to be." He checked the readout on the navigational display.

"The ship ends up where it needs to be?" Hendrix

asked. "The ship? But not you." He studied the navigational array, which was busy calculating the way through the tesseract. "Do you actually fly this ship, or does it do all the work itself?"

Bubbles let out a loud snigger as she glanced at Bronson. "The ship needs to be where it's needed." She focused on Hendrix again, cupping her mouth with her hand as if sharing a secret. "And Bronson is very needy."

"Amasis egress in approximately five point two one space klicks," T-183 announced.

"It took us several cycles to get from Amasis to the nebula. How can we be nearly there now?" Caree asked.

"Time is a bit funny that way."

"Well, hello, handsome," Thalia said in a voice that made Caree's spine tingle with how much she mimicked Iris's old greeting. The cyborg was staring at Hendrix, a haughty smile twisting her lips as if she expected a response.

Caree glanced between Hendrix and the cyborg. His aura was swirling with a mix of colors, predominantly flashes of red and black as he stared at Thalia. Angry. He was angry. It was an unusual tactic for a cyborg to try to psychologically attack someone, but apparently, it had worked. He raised the stasis blaster once again and shot the cyborg, freezing her smug smile in place.

He studied the gun, disgust twisting his lips. "We

need to come up with a permanent way to silence her. This thing doesn't last long, even on full setting."

"I can put her in the medical pod and run a diagnostic subroutine that will keep her asleep for several cycles if needed," T-183 said.

"Good plan," Bronson agreed. "How about you and Remler make that happen before she wakes up again."

"Yes, sir." T-183 and the Rhinernan moved to do as asked. Lifting Thalia between them, they carried her from the main crew area and through a doorway that led to the rest of the ship.

"Cyborgs tend to need to be switched off up here." Bronson tapped his temple with his finger, looking at Hendrix. "Rather than be frozen physically. Why did you bring her? You could've left her for the Core to collect."

"Or blown her up with them," Bubbles added.

"Insurance."

Bronson's eyes widened. "Ooh, sounds like somebody has a plaaan."

"I'm just trying to cover all bases without getting any more of my people killed." Hendrix nodded toward the cargo container full of shifters on the floor in the crew quarters. Gothani and Krystar sat near it, Krystar cradling a blaster at the ready. He didn't trust the situation either. "Once we reach Amasis, they'll need a Stardrive to revive them before they can change into any other form. Then we'll need a home. A habitable planet we can call our own."

"After we free the others, right?" Caree questioned.

"Right." Hendrix nodded at her. "And fight the mind-eaters."

"The what?" Caree asked.

Hendrix shook his head. "Never mind. You've forgotten again. You'll find out soon enough when we get to Amasis. The grays weren't the only reason we needed an army to free the Stardrives."

Caree studied him but couldn't find any indication of him being deceitful. Her sister and friends were being held captive, but the aliens weren't the only threat? The sense that she had forgotten something vital tickled her mind, teasing her memory into recognition. "Oh... oh, yes!" she said as the dimness that clouded her thoughts whenever the mind-eaters were discussed faded. It was part of how they remained hidden in the galaxy, preying upon unsuspecting victims' mental energy. Like Ellie and Axel and the others. How much longer could they survive under constant attack by the parasites? She turned to Bronson. "We need to hurry."

"Yes, we do. Amasis will go into dimensional flux again soon. It will make things quite a bit more difficult if it does so before we've done what we need to do."

"It was becoming unstable when we left it," Hendrix pointed out.

"I don't understand how a planet can exist in different dimensions," Caree said.

"A lot of things do," Bronson said. "But not usually at the same time, which is why as the Stardrive energy decreases on Amasis, it's slowly being pulled apart."

Phoenix squealed and squirmed in Caree's arms. "What?" she asked him. "What is it?"

Instead of replying, he fussed and pushed at her. She should feed him again, but he seemed to want to get down. Maybe a play on the floor would help his restlessness. He was getting so big now. As soon as he was set down, the baby started to crawl in the direction that T-183 and Remler had gone.

"Look at him go!" Marsais clapped her hands. "He's so advanced for a newborn."

"Advanced isn't the word I'd use," Hendrix said.

Caree frowned. Hendrix had never made his distrust of Phoenix a secret. He was scared of the baby and what it might become. And while she understood that the baby's unusual genetic makeup might make people a bit wary of him, he was still her son.

"He's just a baby," she said. "He's different than other babies for sure, but he's still just a baby, and he doesn't deserve to be treated any differently."

"Captain," T-183 called out over the shipboard intercom. "I have found something in the cyborg I think you should see."

Bronson exchanged a wary glance with the others in the room before settling on Hendrix. "Is this a good thing or a bad thing?" he asked over the intercom.

"We don't rightly know," Remler replied. "Which is why we want you to see it."

With Phoenix held protectively in her arms, Caree, Hendrix, Bronson, T-183, and Remler surrounded the flat-bed medical scanner where Thalia lay strapped down. The holographic display floating above her body projected an image of her internal diagnostics.

"Two distinct identities?" Bronson asked.

"Actually, there are three," T-183 said, adjusting the image slightly and zooming in to show the area in Thalia's brain that was of interest. "This one appears to be her original personality that existed before she became a cyborg, but it is within a secured area I cannot access. That is not uncommon in cyborg design as the root personality is often separated to avoid any potential conflicts of interest when the unit is activated for duty. But this is interesting." She shifted the image again, changing the focus to reveal the neural pathways controlling the impulses to and from the cyborg's brain. "There is normally only one identity associated with the command function, but as you can see here..." she pointed at the image where the personality subroutines were displayed, "... you can see quite clearly there is two."

"How is that possible? And what does it mean?" Bronson asked.

Remler shrugged and looked at Bronson. "We were hoping you could tell us."

"Best guess..." T-183 said, then continued, "... judging by the messy integration, is that a second personality was copied over the first, without deleting any of the original personality programming."

"If Thalia belongs to Rose, she must know, right?" Caree pointed out. "But why do something like that?"

"I do not have enough information to assess that," T-183 said.

Bronson peered at the image closely. "More interesting question, I think, is who are the identities? The original we can assume is unchanged as it's partitioned off in a secure area, but these other two... is one dominant and the other recessive? Could it be her primary identity has become damaged and split?"

"It is unlikely." T-183 shook her head. "Her functioning does not show signs of decay or damage in that manner."

"Two people in one body. I understand it now." Caree closed her eyes as Phoenix kicked his legs, bouncing in her arms. "I feel them both. Familiar and unfamiliar. They are entwined."

"It's Iris," Hendrix said quietly.

"Yes!" Caree agreed. It made sense now the way the cyborg had greeted Hendrix using Iris's familiar saying. Even if she hadn't felt the two identities inside the cyborg, the fact that Thalia switched personalities in an incredibly non-cyborg manner without seeming to realize was a key indication that something wasn't right. "It's Iris and Thalia, mixed together." Caree opened her eyes and glanced at the mercenary. His face was unreadable as he stared at the cyborg strapped onto the medical scanner. "Is it the whole of her identity?" she asked T-183.

"Uncertain," said the cyborg. "But two identities form unique patterns that overlap."

"Thalia killed Iris," Hendrix said. "Then Axel's brother, Kendrick, shot Thalia. She was damaged. We left her in the Borbian prison."

"Where Iris had been kept in a virtual cage for months," Bronson added. "But how did a copy of her end up inside Rosamunde Cruz's pet cyborg, and why?"

"That's something we need to ask Rose," Hendrix said. "Is it possible to separate the identities?" he asked T-183.

"Possible, yes. However, it would require extensive surgical programming and not be without risk. Some areas may be unable to separate. The identities could be irreparably damaged."

Hendrix studied the Thalia slash Iris cyborg in silence. The relationship he'd had with the pirate wasn't what Caree would've considered a love bond, but perhaps she had meant more to him than she had understood. Shifters were not a species she was familiar with for their mating practices or social connections. However, Hendrix did seem loyal to his people. Perhaps that loyalty extended to others as well if he became attached to his need of them. His human form did seem to influence his shifter personality.

"Does she pose any kind of threat?" Bronson asked.

"Not currently," T-183 said. "She has been artificially induced into an unconscious state and will not awaken unless given the command to do so."

"Good." Bronson nodded, seeming satisfied. "Keep her asleep for now. We can decide what to do with her after we've completed the mission on

Amasis, which we're arriving at...." he glanced at his wrist comm, "... right about now."

"We've arrived at the Amasis system, Bronson," Bubbles called out over the ship's intercom.

"See?" Bronson said with the cocky grin Caree had come to expect from him. His aura was hard to read, but he never seemed to lack confidence. "Prepare the slip drive," he said over the comm to Bubbles.

"Frelling shit." The Travanian's voice carried her customary disgust. "I knew you were going to say that. Everyone better grab something to vomit in. I'm not cleaning the mess this time."

12

Axel blinked. In the dim lighting of the cell, it was hard to make out the others. Ellie lay beside him, chains about her wrists and ankles restricting her movements. His own clinked as he shifted, trying to find a more comfortable position on the hard floor, but just like every other time he'd tried to relax, it was impossible. His skin was chaffed from the heavy metal bands encircling his limbs and weighing on him. His body was bruised in places he didn't even know he could get bruised. And his mind—it was hard to say how damaged his mind was—but he was certain it wasn't working normally any longer. How many days had it been now? Time was one long moment of sliding further into the abyss between reality and the nightmare fantasy that was the real prison that trapped them.

Kendrick and Shiznit were nearby, wearing chains the same as he and Ellie. Their eyes were closed, but while Shiznit remained still, Kendrick was rolling and thrashing and kicking, creating discordant music of clinking metal and nightmare moans, which added to the distress that twisted at Axel's insides.

Helpless to wake him, he understood what his oldest brother was going through. The visions were getting worse for everyone, apart from Shiznit. Why was it that the Gho'bar didn't suffer like the rest of them did?

Ellie shook her head and rested it on her arms as she looked at Axel. Her face was pale in the dimness, but he didn't need to see her clearly to know her tiredness. "This is going to kill us," she said.

Axel nodded. Uncle Henry sat against the wall with his knees almost against his chest, his head bowed, and his hands covering his ears, trying to block out the noise and visions. The man had traded one prison experience for another. How much longer before his already fragile mind fractured completely? How much longer could any of them remain sane?

Maybe it would be easier not to be sane and simply forget there ever was anything besides this cell and whatever nightmares the Amasis aliens continued to inflict on all of them. Why were they doing this? Axel tried to remember, but it was as if his mind was coated in oil, slippery and unreliable to hold.

Hendrix. It was Hendrix's fault, wasn't it? He'd escaped and left them all here like the coward that he was. Wasn't he? No, he'd left to go get help. Axel remembered now. He was the only one who could fight. The oil slicked his mind again, making it hard to think but leaving him with the impression that Hendrix was the key to something important. "We have to trust him," he said out loud more to remind himself than anyone else.

"Who? Hendrix?" Ellie asked. "Yeah, not gonna happen." She rolled from her side onto her back and folded her arms. "He kidnapped my sister and her newborn baby and left us here to rot."

"Caree will come back, even if he doesn't. If you can't trust him, trust her."

"She's just had a baby. She's vulnerable. Who the hell knows what that asshole will do to her, let alone that poor baby."

Axel tried finding a comfortable position again but was as unsuccessful as before. "Listen. I know it's hard to trust that it will be okay, but we have to keep believing it will be." Hope was the only thing keeping them all from sinking into complete despair, and he knew it. "He'll come back with Caree and the reinforcements he promised."

"When?"

"When the time is right. He has no way to contact us without the grays knowing. And they'll know the plan is for him to come back for us."

"Which makes me even more nervous," Ellie said. "And have you seen the way the guards treat us in comparison?"

"In comparison to who?" Axel asked, confused by her words.

Ellie stared for a few seconds and shook her head. "Never mind."

Axel's pulse increased. Her mind was beginning to become affected by the constant exposure to the abusive dreams they kept having. He'd insist that she be left alone and beg the grays take whatever they wanted from him instead if he could. He had done so many times, he was sure. But whatever it was that they wanted by forcing them to endure the nightmare visions that seemed so real was something they wanted from all of them. But it wasn't the grays doing this, was it? There was something more even they were afraid of.

Kendrick stopped moving, filling the cell with abrupt silence. He lay still for a long moment, but unlike Shiznit, Kendrick's chest didn't seem to be rising.

"Kendrick?" Axel stared at his brother, waiting to see some signs of life. A moan. A whimper. Something. Anything. But his brother remained still as death. "Kendrick!" Axel yelled.

His brother didn't respond, even as Shiznit shifted and rolled on his side but didn't wake.

Axel looked at Ellie. This was bad. Kendrick was the strong one, the one who could take anything. Axel stood and walked as close to the two-way mirror on the side of their cell as his chain would allow. He looked into the mirror, but the only thing he could see was the shadowy reflection of himself staring back.

"Hey!" he shouted. "You need to get in here now! My brother isn't well." He continued to yell at his reflection in the mirror, not sure if any of the grays, blues, purples, or whoever else might be on the other side were listening or not, but why have a mirror like this if not to watch them?

The doorway to their cell remained closed. The lights didn't come on. The only sound in the room was Shiznit's light snoring and Uncle Henry's mumbles while he talked to himself and kept his forehead pressed to his knees.

Axel walked as close to his brother as he could. "Kendrick, are you okay?"

Ellie placed her hand on Axel's shoulder and wrapped her arms around him. "I'm so sorry, Axel. He's gone."

No, no way. There was no possible chance that his brother, the big tough guy, could be gone. Not like this. "Kendrick!" he yelled as loud as he could. The sound should've echoed around the room like a roar, but instead, there was only silence.

He clutched at his throat, but no sound would

come out. Axel turned to Ellie.

She was no longer chained to the wall but standing beside him. "It's okay, Axel. I'll see if I can wake him."

"Ellie?" he called out, but no sound passed his lips.

She smiled as she stood above Kendrick and looked down at him. "I think I know what he needs. You Ryans are all the same."

"Ellie!" Axel screamed soundlessly as she crouched down on her knees beside Kendrick and slowly unzipped the top of her flight suit. Axel reached for her, but now he could no longer move. All he could do was watch in mute horror while Ellie pushed the top of her suit down, revealing the pale skin of her neck and chest. A loose bandage covered the vein on her neck, where it met her collarbone. She peeled it off and smiled as a fresh trickle of blood began to flow down her chest from the tiny twin puncture wounds that pierced her otherwise flawless skin.

She touched the blood with her index finger and smiled. "You were hungry before," she said to Axel. "But I have enough for him."

She traced her finger against Kendrick's pale lips, painting them red with her blood. His eyes opened almost immediately, and his tongue flicked out, tasting the crimson salvation that she offered.

He wasn't dead. He wasn't unconscious. No, no.

This was worse. He was a vampire. But then so was he, wasn't he? Seeing Ellie's bright red blood caused a pang of hunger to rip through Axel, so fierce it was painful. Ellie was his. His mate. His food. He couldn't let Kendrick have her too.

"Ellie, no!" Axel screamed in silence, but it was already too late. Kendrick was on her instantly, pulling her down to him, his mouth finding her neck and his hands holding her in place while he bit and sucked and ravaged the life-giving sustenance from her.

"Come join us, Axel." Ellie moaned as she raised her free hand weakly beckoning him, her urgent gaze finding his as she clutched Kendrick's head to her neck, stroking his long hair now stained in red. "It feels so good," she said. "But not as good as with you."

Kendrick kept on sucking and licking blood from her exposed vein for several moments while Axel stood watching the love of his life writhe and moan until Ellie's enjoyment increased to the point where she passed out for a second. But Kendrick seemed oblivious to how pale she was becoming and kept on sucking. Ellie gripped his hair when she came to, the blissful smile on her lips twitching into a frown. "You're okay now. It's enough." She tried to push him aside to no avail. Her hands did nothing but bat at him weakly.

Her gaze met Axel's again. "Help me," she pleaded.

"Why aren't you saving her?" Uncle Henry asked, looking at Axel. "Didn't I teach you anything?" The old man flashed his fangs. "She's your bond-mate, but instead, you let your savage brother have her." Henry shook his head. "You're an insult to the name of Ryan, boy. She doesn't deserve you."

Uncle Henry positioned himself beside Kendrick and Ellie. She was moaning more strongly now, even as her body was losing strength. Kendrick was drinking too much, too fast, and there wasn't anything Axel could do about it.

"I'll finish the job quickly, don't worry, dear," Uncle Henry said as he pierced the flesh of her left wrist with his fangs and began to suck her blood too.

Ellie's eyes shut as she cried out weakly, "Axel?"

"No!" Axel screamed, but all he could do was watch in silence. His mind was shaking with rage and despair. Unable to move. Unable to speak. Blood was thundering through his veins as Ellie's own was drained by his brother and uncle, leaving her pale, empty and lifeless as the endless nightmare they were trapped in continued.

13

Using the Bohemia's slip drive to pass through the chronotron particle barrier that surrounded Amasis had been the easy part, Hendrix mused as he watched the rainbow-hued clouds part while they slipped through the atmosphere. Even the headache and nausea that plagued him and the others as aftereffects of slipping within space-time was something he could handle. It would pass, but landing the ship in a place where there were Stardrives without an army of mind-eaters around, was going to be tricky. The shifters held in the cargo container needed to feed before they could fight. If the mind-eaters swarmed them before they were ready, they would be easy prey.

Bronson frowned as he glanced at the navigation console. "T, have you got a reading on a Stardrive energy signature?"

"There are many. Sending the coordinates for

the nearest now," T-183 said.

Caree's gaze was fixed on the main viewscreen while Phoenix was wrapped in her arms and held tight to her chest. "This is a different way than what we took," she said. "Last time we crashed. I think."

"The multi-phasic shielding is currently protecting us," Bronson declared. "But there's a great deal of unstable energy due to the dimensional flux."

"This planet is frelled," Bubbles muttered, looking at the topographic telemetry. "I estimate we have approximately twenty-four hours at most before it goes completely tits-up and either pulls us with it into another dimension or pulls itself apart. And judging by the level of instability in the core, it's set to blow."

Hendrix crossed his arms over his chest. "Great. We're landing on a ticking time bomb."

"A ticking time bomb where our friends are held captive." Caree's tone was heavy with censure as she stared at him.

"And all the Stardrives," he reminded her. Two could play the my-stakes-are-bigger-than-yours game. He was getting tired of her not-so-subtle accusations that he wouldn't be true to his word and use the shifters to rescue the others. Bah, who cared what she thought? He'd made his priorities evident from the start.

"We need to become fully phased with this

timeline if we want to interact with the planet," Bronson called out to the others. "Which means we need to lower the temporal shielding. Keep yourselves strapped in," he instructed. "This ride is about to get very bumpy."

"Adjusting our temporal signature to match that of Amasis," Remler called out.

Bronson nodded. He grabbed the ship's controls and held them tight in his grasp. As the shielding adapted, a greenish cloud surrounded them, and a strong electromagnetic force gripped the ship, causing it to shake as they connected with the unstable atmosphere.

Sitting beside Hendrix in the passenger seating, Caree gasped as the ship flipped to its side and slipped through a gap between the green cloud and a red one. The whole ship vibrated as the ionic energy they passed through heated the hull, causing a discharge of superheated particles to arc between the clouds and the ship. Bronson hit the thrusters and shot the Queen Bohemia lower into Amasis's atmosphere. Within seconds, they were below the cloud layer and into the open sky where the sun was setting into dusk.

"There's nothing there." Marsais pointed at the front viewport as the clouds parted. The planet's surface was gray—no mountains, no gullies—nothing but gray soil for as far as the eye could see. A baren landscape of clay that Hendrix had become all too familiar with.

"Oh no," Caree said. "There's plenty. It depends on where you are."

"There." Phoenix pointed at a spot on the holographic navigational map where the clay fields gave way to lush plant life. "We need to go there," he said in his high-pitched baby voice.

Hendrix stared at him. "Oh great, the freak speaks in complete sentences now?"

The baby looked at him. "Asshole."

"Phoenix!" Caree shouted. "I told you before not to use that word. It's bad."

"Kid is not wrong," Bubbles murmured.

Hendrix shook his head as the baby calmly popped its thumb into its mouth and clung to its mother in an expression of innocence that the mercenary was certain was feigned. The kid was a little freak, all right. No way was he falling for the he's-just-a-really-special-baby nonsense.

"Stardrive energy signature directly ahead, Captain," T-183 announced. "It appears to be a nest of them."

"Let's hope it's not a nest of the mind-eaters as well." Hendrix's words were greeted with confused stares. Frell. How were they supposed to win this fight if the weak-minded solids couldn't even remember what they were fighting? "The invisible boogeymen that have infected this planet..." he said matter-of-factly, "... and feed off your brains."

Bronson blinked. "Right. Yes. Once we've landed, we'll take the cargo container outside to the Stardrives so the shifters can feed directly once released. If we extend the ship's shielding, it should help protect us from the mind-eaters for a few minutes if any are in the vicinity."

Hendrix nodded. "Might work." Probably not, but they were short on options, regardless.

Bronson gave a quick nod and turned his attention to the cyborg. "T, I want you and Remler to stay on board and work on Thalia. See what else you can discover about her and if we can use it to our advantage."

"Yes, Captain," she replied.

"The rest of you..." Bronson glanced around the ship's small crew, "... are with me." The grin he flashed was quick and bright. "Let's kick some invisible boogeyman ass."

As it turned out, Hendrix's concern about being attacked by the mind-eaters while the shifters fed and regained their strength had been for nothing. Bronson's trick with extending the shields had worked without a problem. In the fading light of Amasis's day, he looked at the crowd of eighty-seven Memini, the last of his species. He'd done what was necessary to get them this far. Now they needed to fight for their future in the galaxy.

"What the frell is this?" one of the shifters, Gothani, asked as she kneeled by one of the withered vines that had once nurtured many Stardrives.

The Queen Bohemia had landed near a small area of towering, blue-stemmed plant life, which glowed faintly in the growing darkness. The Stardrives were attached to vines nestled protectively amongst the stems. The spherical balls of energy should have been robust and glowing with health. A small growth of six Stardrives like this should've been capable of sustaining the energy needs of several worlds for millennia if they were taken care of and maintained. And just one of the orbs should have had more than enough resources to revitalize all the shifters without depleting its store of energy. But the cluster of Stardrives, which had been barely glowing when they had arrived, were now dark and desiccated, the vines withered and thin.

Caree and Phoenix bent closer to a Stardrive attached to the vine that had once nurtured it. The baby had just finished feeding from it and was now glowing with a steady blue light. He was the brightest light source in the grove now that the Stardrives had gone dark. He pressed his fingers into the skin surrounding the Stardrive. The casing gave way with a 'pop,' rupturing the orb and releasing the scent of decay and a trickle of thick liquid. Phoenix jerked his hand back, and he started to cry.

Caree wrapped her arms around the child and hugged him tightly. "It's okay," she said softly, soothing him. "It's okay." Except it wasn't okay. The Stardrives had given the last of their energy to feed them all.

"Eew," Marsais placed her hand over her nose. "I've never seen them do that before."

"You've seen a lot of Stardrives up close, have you?" Bubbles asked, her tone filled with her usual bite.

"I didn't know they looked like that when they died," Marsais explained. "I've only ever seen them explode."

"Well, we're going to die if we don't get out of here soon," said Bubbles. She raised her laser rifle and sighted through it as she scanned the grove, her expression grim.

"It's worse than that," Gothani said. "So many Stardrives... the heart of our life in the galaxy. If they all die, how will we live?" She rose and looked at Hendrix. "We need to get as many healthy ones on board the ship as we can and take them with us. They can't be left here to wither and rot, sucked dry by the mind-eaters."

"That's what I told you before on the Millennial ship. But now you believe me?" He shook his head and didn't wait for her response. He knew the truth. "We'll need a bigger ship to transport them." He pulled up his wrist comm and activated his scanner. "This hangar is where we left from before. It's filled with ships." He scanned the contents of the hangar, isolating a large cargo vessel that he remembered seeing and appeared to be in good repair. "This one might do." He glanced at Gothani and then Bronson. "We'll split into teams. "Caree, Bronson, and your crew can take charge of rescuing Axel and the others. Gothani, take a team and start collecting the healthiest Stardrives that can be salvaged. Bring them to the ship for transport, and don't forget the vines so they can be transplanted." Was it possible to transplant Stardrives? He'd only ever seen them used as an energy source, but eons ago, they had once grown on his home planet as well as others. Maybe they could again.

"What about the mind-eaters," Gothani asked. "As soon as we start moving Stardrives around, they'll focus the fight on us. We'll be squatting dicks."

"I believe you mean, 'sitting ducks,'" Bronson interjected with a quick grin.

Hendrix nodded. "The rest of us will act as a shield against the mind-eaters and kill as many of the felling parasites as we can."

Gothani gave him a curt nod, for once not arguing with him about what to do.

"Guys, we really need to get moving," Remler announced over the comm from the ship. "The instability of this planet is increasing. We have fewer hours instead of more hours if you catch my drift."

"Right. Let's do this." Bronson clapped Hendrix on the back. "We'll meet you at the cargo ship. T-183?" he called into his wrist comm. "Return the shields to normal but keep the engines hot. We'll need to leave in a hurry. Things are about to get exciting."

"That's one word for it," Bubbles muttered.

"Yes, Captain," the cyborg called out over the comm.

"So where do we go?" Marsais asked, looking between Bronson and Caree.

"We need to find the way into the main facility," Caree said. "The others are held in a room there."

"Over there." Phoenix pointed, indicating a gap in the stems, opposite the direction where the Bohemia waited. He kicked his legs. "Put me down," he instructed Caree. She did as he wanted, keeping one of her hands in his.

"That baby is adorable," Marsais said. "Plovanians grow very quickly but nothing like this."

"He's special." Bronson smiled. "Let's do as he

says. He senses things on a level we can't." The group traveled in the direction that Phoenix walked, leaving the shifters to look out into the darkness to do battle.

As soon as the Bohemia's shields retracted, leaving them exposed to Amasis, the group of shifters looked at Hendrix, their expressions growing tense. "I can feel them," one of the newly revived shifters said, assuming a fighting stance and glancing at the empty air about them.

Hendrix nodded. He could feel them, too—a prickling on the back of his neck. He wasn't going to fall for their game this time. "We're vulnerable to them like this. Turn into the next thing I do. It will help you battle them easier than in these human skins." He focused on the image in his mind, allowing his body to shake and take on a new shape in a blur of rapid activity. His arms transformed into wings, and the rest of his body thinned out, becoming the lizard-like form of a Pterodon. As the rest followed suit, the grove became filled with the beating of leathery wings and the screech of bird-like squawking.

"Will this work?" one of the shifters asked.

Hendrix flexed his sharp talons where his feet had been. "It has to." He'd used this form before to scout out the landscape with Ellie. It would allow them to move quickly and gather Stardrives, which they could carry in the leather pouches the species normally used for protecting offspring. The sharp, predatory claws reminded him of Iris and the poison-tipped glove she used to have. She had been deadly when she used it. He'd be even deadlier now. He launched into the dark sky, using the creature's night vision to seek out any movement that might indicate they had company. "Come on, you scumbags, come and get us." His challenge shrieked out, echoing off the distant hillside, acting as a rallying cry for the others to follow him.

A chilling high-pitched squeal filled the air in answer. The shifters broke into small groups, each forming a 'V' pattern, leaving enough room for beating wings and sharp claws.

"It's great to be alive again," one of the shifters yelled as they soared high into the night, free of the constraints of the wingless. Hendrix screeched in agreement. When was the last time the galaxy had seen an event like this? Eighty-odd Memini all fighting together. The mind-eaters didn't stand a chance.

Below them, the ground appeared like the endless flat plain of clay dotted with an occasional grove of stems. The lusher areas would contain the groves and burrows where the Stardrives were grown. "Head for the hills," he called out to Gothani. "Gather as many Stardrives as you can. We'll cover you."

With a screech, she broke away from the main

group and headed in the direction of the distant hillside, taking ten of the shifters with her.

As Hendrix covered her from above, the air temperature lowered. A lightning-quick blur passed in front of him, but he was quicker. Banking sideways, he swung his claws in a diagonal slash, drawing blood from the unseen contact. "Bring it on," he said.

He could see them easier like this. Feel their presence. The prickle at the back of his skull indicated they were trying to gain access to his mind.

Frell that.

As he spun and cut through the air, the other shifters did likewise, and the gray soil far beneath their wings became splattered in crimson liquid and pools of dark blood as mind eater after mind eater was carved to pieces, their form becoming visible as they died. As a group, the shifters were like a well-oiled machine—slicing, dicing, and bringing down the parasites with cool precision. Hundreds of them. Thousands. The planet was infested, but the shifters were pest control.

"Oh yes, it's great to be alive again," one of the shifters shouted and let out a huge screeching laugh.

"Last time to get to the main facility, we took an elevator in one of the giant stems that went up, not down," Caree said. "Are you sure we're going the right way?" she asked Phoenix.

The baby nodded, seeming determined to push all the buttons and levers in the elevator car at the same time.

"It's probably this one, little guy." Bronson pushed a green button that was lit and positioned too high on the wall console for the baby to reach.

Phoenix squealed in excitement as the car started moving. Caree grasped his hand in hers, using her other one to clutch the railing for support.

Phoenix had led Caree, Bronson, and the crew of the Bohemia to a crevasse in the ground which, when stepped into, had revealed a metal platform that had turned out to be the beginning of an underground elevator system.

"Did you know about this place?" Caree asked Bronson.

"The planet or the elevator?"

"The planet. The elevator. Everything." Being a time traveler, he probably knew many things. He always seemed to be aware of events that she didn't, not even as an empath.

He shrugged and crossed his arms over his chest, causing his long black jacket to rustle and the bottom hem to swish, creating a new thing for Phoenix to be fascinated with. "We knew of the planet, but I've never had a reason to come here before."

"It isn't all like this..." Caree stated, then continued, "... all gray and drab. There are also vines and forests and rivers and hills. At least, parts I've seen. But I think the Stardrives have been drained so much the Amasisans can't keep it up. It was probably quite beautiful once and full of life." There was a sad desperation about Amasis as if the planet knew it was dying. She'd be glad when they were away from it again. The constant strain and stress of the emotions flying around was difficult to process, not to mention the danger to Phoenix. She had no doubt the grays would try to kidnap and keep them in here again.

"I can't make sense of any of this." Bubbles twisted the image projected from her wrist scanner around, frowning at it. "The tunnel we're in isn't listed on here. Are we even moving?"

"Oh, we're moving all right." Bronson smiled as Phoenix smacked a wet handprint on his jacket, giggling at the sound it made.

"I don't like this. Are you sure we aren't heading into a trap?" Marsais asked.

"Quite possibly," Bronson said. "But then again,

maybe not."

"Oh, that's reassuring," Bubbles muttered.

"There are at least two versions of Amasis in existence, the one you see now and the one you see when the planet fluxes," Bronson explained. "Which one we're in differs depending on the time."

"This is making my head ache." Bubbles growled in frustration. "Which frelling reality are we in?"

The elevator jolted as it came to a sudden stop. When the door opened, all that was visible was the same expanse of gray clay and darkness they had seen before getting on the elevator.

"Did we even go anywhere?" Marsais bent and touched the ground with a gloved hand. Her fingers appeared to sink into it, and the indentation she created caused the ground to ripple like a stone had been dropped into a pond. "What is this place?" Marsais asked, standing. She brushed her fingers against her thigh, trying to wipe away any dirt that clung to her glove. As she did so, the rippling spread from the ground and into the darkness, causing the air around them to shimmer and distort with increasing velocity until it suddenly dissolved into an entirely different view.

"What the frell?" Bubbles shook her head as if to clear it.

"What just happened?" Marsais asked simultaneously.

"Dimensional flux," Bronson stated matter-of-factly.

Caree clutched Phoenix's hand, feeling slightly dizzy and disoriented, but the baby grinned, seeming unaffected by the abrupt change of scenery. He tugged her out of the elevator and into what now appeared to be a dimly lit, gigantic room, devoid of any lifeforms or the ships Caree remembered being there.

It was the hangar bay that Hendrix, Phoenix, and she had left from a couple of weeks prior, only now it appeared desolate and abandoned.

"It's changed," Caree said. "We weren't gone that long. There were many ships and gray aliens everywhere."

"We took too long." Marsais shook her head.

"No. We're seeing what they want us to see," Phoenix explained in his squeaky baby voice. He toddled forward on his tiny legs, aiming for a corridor across the room, which Caree remembered led to the area where they had been imprisoned.

"That baby—" Marsais started.

"*Is* growing too quickly. Yes, I know, but he was born for something special." Caree increased her pace to keep up with Phoenix. "He was born in a room not far from here. We're closer to the others than we think."

The lights in the cavernous room cut out, leaving

them in total darkness. Caree froze, clutching Phoenix's hand in hers.

"Don't fear the darkness, Mama." The baby's small voice seemed loud in the room. "Only fear what your brain tells you. What you're about to see isn't real." Phoenix's small hand gripped hers tightly. "They have found us."

"Who has?" she whispered, almost afraid to speak.

"The mind-eaters," Phoenix said. *'Don't be scared, Mama. I'll keep us safe,'* he added through their empathic connection.

Despite his reassuring thoughts, Caree's skin prickled as the temperature inside the room plummeted. She could see nothing but darkness, but as she stared, she swore something slithered around in the room, just on the edge of her hearing.

"Something's in here," Bubbles whispered. She readied her blaster as did Bronson and Marsais, the guns being cocked, making an audible click. Caree felt rather than saw Phoenix raise his tiny hand and shake his head.

"Don't," the baby warned. "They feed on your fear."

"What's out there?" Marsais whispered.

"The creatures that Hendrix and the shifters are fighting. We can't see them, but they'll stop at nothing, and the more vivid your visions, the more it feeds them," Caree explained. "I recognize this feeling. We need to keep moving toward the others despite what we see. They'll make us forget why we're here."

"Is there anything you can do, Bronson?" Marsais asked.

His coat rustled as he shrugged. "We're travelers, not wizards. Can you tell where to go, Phoenix?"

"Yes," the baby answered without hesitation. "Must hurry."

"Let's get moving," Caree said. "Try not to think."

"That's easy for Marsais," Bubbles said as they shuffled forward in the darkness. Even Phoenix's natural blue glow couldn't penetrate the gloom that clouded their vision, which reminded her how effective the mind-eaters' tricks were. The baby likely was glowing, she just couldn't see it. The hangar was probably still filled with ships, judging by how Phoenix seemed to be guiding them around things instead of taking a straight line. Or maybe this was all in her mind? Maybe they had already succumbed and were lying in a cell somewhere being fed on. The last time they'd had a Stardrive protecting them, they had made their way to a ship and escaped. There was nothing to do this time except try to remain calm and not give into the fear that clutched at her heart and whispered in her mind. They wanted her baby. Her child. She should've left him on the ship and not brought him with her this far.

'No, Mama. I need to be here. It's okay,' Phoenix told her telepathically. '*Trust me.*' But his words did nothing to still her racing heart and mind.

She clutched his tiny hand as he led them steadily onward into the black nothingness that surrounded them. What kind of a mother was she? What kind of a mother would put her child in so much danger? He was just a baby—still an infant despite his advanced abilities. She should be protecting him, not the other way around. She was a failure and a disgrace.

A loud hiss echoed throughout the room. "The child, give us the child," a harsh voice demanded as if carried around the area by wind and wrapping around Caree's mind. The scream building inside her stuck in her throat.

"No! We can't do that," Bronson shouted, stepping close to the baby. "You'll have to come through us."

Phoenix's hand clutched Caree's. The energy that flowed from her son to the surroundings tapped into her reserves as well, creating a moment of dizziness. The invisible enemies were here, and given Phoenix's amplified abilities, he'd be their main target, but it appeared he knew that already and had come prepared. She could see the images flipping through his head, faster and faster, almost blinding her to try and look at them all. She wanted to protect her son—just a baby—but her baby was remarkably strong.

Phoenix let go of her hand and sat on the floor, putting his hands on his temples. Light filled the room so suddenly it was as if it had been switched on. Caree blinked, trying to regain her bearings, noting the others did the same. A buzz lightly echoed as the electrical systems rebooted, or maybe it was her mind, because the cold that had surrounded her, filling her with doubts and fears, was gone. The hanger was much like she remembered it from before when she'd left Amasis with Hendrix, filled with ships of various types and sizes and a group of the gray-skinned Watchers, doing exactly as they usually did—watching.

"You've returned," one of them said to Caree. "And the child."

She didn't like the way they looked at Phoenix. Their auras were filled with a mixture of emotions, making them hard to read. But she didn't trust them any more than she trusted the mind-eaters. Or shifters.

"We came for my sister and my friends." Caree moved to stand in front of Phoenix. "And if you try to stop us or steal my baby again, I'll let these three people holding the guns kill you."

A blue-skinned alien stepped out from behind the group of grays. "You must not interfere. You will remain here until it is time."

The blue alien turned to walk away. "Hey!" Caree called out. "What about my friends?"

"You will see them soon."

The grays turned and left, following the blue. Caree looked down at Phoenix, then at Bronson. "What do we do?"

"I guess we wait," Bronson said. "Time is one of those things that you just don't play with."

"Really?" Bubbles rolled her eyes. "Like you never do that."

"What we could really use right now..." Bronson ran his hand through his hair, "... is a Stardrive."

"I agree." Caree studied her baby and frowned. Phoenix was so tired he sagged, his hands dropping to his sides. Caree immediately picked him up and cradled him in her arms. He needed to replenish his energy. A Stardrive could do that better than she, but they didn't have the luxury of a Stardrive this time. She unzipped the top of her flight suit and gave him her breast to feed. "He can't keep this up. And neither can we. He drove off the mind-eaters, but they'll be back. The grays want Phoenix. They can't have him if he's with me. But if the mind-eaters incapacitate me, and Phoenix is too weak to drive them away, that will give the grays their chance to take him. We need to get to the others before that. I'm not waiting any longer."

Not caring to see if Bronson and the others followed, she headed for the door the grays had exited through, feeding Phoenix as best as she could while she walked.

"Axel, hold me," Ellie said to him. She lay on a hospital bed, a team of medical staff gathered to help her give birth.

Axel put his hand in Ellie's. Her grip immediately tightened, causing pain to race through his hand and up his arm, making it impossible not to wince. He had heard that while giving birth, a female human gained the strength of a dozen Travanians, and he was pretty sure that wasn't true. He was certain that the number should be closer to a hundred.

Ellie screamed.

"You've got this, baby," he said.

"Don't call me, baby!" she yelled, then screamed again as she continued to work to give birth.

"Yes, come on, push that baby out and give it to Nana," a voice said from behind Axel. He turned to see the speaker and froze for a second. Rosamunde Cruz. Ellie's mother.

"What are you doing here?" Axel asked.

"Reminding you that you can never escape me."

Her words chilled him as the head of his new

baby girl emerged, but something was wrong. Ellie's face had turned white, and her expression slackened instead of the grimace it had been. As the doctor pulled the baby free, Ellie didn't scream or cry. He couldn't feel the strength of her grip any longer.

"Ellie wasn't strong enough, and neither are you." Rose's words penetrated his mind at the same time as the cold steel of a long blade pierced his back. Looking down, he stared in mute horror as his knees grew weak, and the tip of the blade protruded from the front of his chest.

Axel sat up straight. He wiped the sweat from his brow and looked at the bars of his cage. He turned to Shiznit, sleeping peacefully on the rock-hard ground and obviously not suffering from horrible nightmares like his. Ellie lay nearby, sleeping in her cage, clearly not dead and no sign of having given birth to a baby.

Axel felt his chest with his fingers, remembering the vivid pain of the blade piercing his flesh.

So real.

It was always so real.

"We need to get out of this place," he said out loud.

"We need a Stardrive," Ellie said in her sleep. "They need to feed."

The shifter to Hendrix's right suffered a cut to its left wing—a long gash that rendered the limb useless. The shifter spiraled down to the ground, continuing the fight on foot as best it could by shifting into a Monsatan. Three of its gun arms fired at what appeared to be empty air, at times seeming to hit one of the invisible targets swarming the area. But the fourth arm hung limp. More energy was needed to heal the damaged limb no matter what form the shifter might take. But they were here to save what Stardrives they could, not drain them of their life energy. Gothani and her team had managed to secure a few and were en-route with them to the cargo ship, but most were weak, and what energy they had needed to be preserved for their future instead was being used now.

But if they didn't get off the planet, would it even matter?

"Those things have sharp claws, don't let them get close," Hendrix warned them all again with a loud screech. But the warnings didn't help when outnumbered like they were, no matter how many mind-eaters they carved down. The idea of mind-eaters having claws was an effective hallucination as it was also the one thing that would harm the shifters in their flying form. The mind-eaters were clever, playing on the natural fear instinct of the Pterodons' primitive brain. Hendrix had tried to override instinct with rational thinking, but it hadn't done a damn thing. And if they shifted to any other form, the mind-eaters would just use whatever primal fear lurked in the brain to create a weakness to prey upon.

"I take back what I said, I'd rather be back in a deep sleep," one of the shifters said.

The air grew cold, causing Hendrix's breath to become a visible mist as one of the mind-eaters flew closely past him. Hendrix turned to attack it, following the blur that registered in his Pterodon night vision toward the ground where the Monsatan-shifter was now surrounded and flailing wildly. Hendrix banked his wings and pushed forward with his talons, the sharp nails going deep inside his invisible target and freeing the shifter by creating a gap in the swarm surrounding him.

The shifter acted quickly, slipping through the gap and forming a protective wall back to back with Hendrix, at least reducing one area of attack against them. However, it did nothing to stop the assault, and the Monsatan lost another arm to the deadly invisible claw attack.

"Is there no end to these things?" the Monsatan-shifter shrieked. He was in pain. Hendrix knew he must be but had no way to assist except to keep slicing the air with his talons and hope he hit something more than he missed.

"There has to be," Hendrix said. He paused for only a split second as the air filled with the spray of warm blood from his latest kill, but it was enough time for one of the enemies to swipe across his chest with their razor-sharp claws. Blood spurted from where the scaled hide had been cleaved, and he instinctively shifted into his usual human form so he could place a hand across his chest to try to slow down the bleeding.

"Change form again," one of the others shouted. "You're a sitting duck like that."

"I can't, I'm too injured." Blood seeped between Hendrix's fingers even as he pressed down hard on the severed skin to stop the wound from leaking his precious life energy.

The remainder of the shifters surrounded him to keep him safe from further attacks. He closed his eyes and slowed down his breathing. After a few heartbeats, the pressure inside his chest slowly lifted. He took a few minutes to take it easy, watching his fellow shifters slice their way through the enemy, grateful for their defense.

One of the shifters fell to the ground clutching his neck. The shifter changed to a humanoid form and put his hands up to his throat to stop the blood from spurting. But the mind-eaters on the ground who Hendrix had thought were severed bodies of dead meat, grabbed at the shifter, several pairs of hands digging at his body and limbs, bringing him down in a screaming gush of blood.

Hendrix blinked. What was this? What was this now? More illusion? Had the mind-eaters infiltrated his mind in his weakened state? He had somehow fallen and was lying on the ground, looking up at the night sky that was filled with shrieks and cries and the bitter metallic tang of blood. He put his hands to the ground and forced his body to cooperate and rise.

The scene around him caused his stomach to clench. Shifters were everywhere, some wounded, some fighting, but the mind-eaters outnumbered them. Bodies from both sides covered the clay plain now slick with dark blood. And to his horror, some of the bodies were rising. Shifters who had fallen during the fight slowly getting back up again, limbs missing and wounds dripping blood, turning against their own kind. A mind eater trick for sure, but how? And how to fight it without being sure they weren't killing themselves?

One of the shifters surrounding him while he recovered bent down to try to pull a near-dead reanimated shifter into safety, but Hendrix shook his head. "He's gone!" he yelled. "Leave them, or you'll die too."

Zombies. Where were the mind-eaters getting that horror from? His humanoid brain?

Another shifter body hit the ground, followed by its head seemingly cut clean from its neck due to the sharpness of the mind-eater's claws. This was a hopeless task.

"Regroup," Hendrix shouted. He hoped feverishly there was enough time to come up with a new plan that would work. Or this fight was going to be over quickly.

14

Tobias Cruz had no idea why Blake Bronson had stranded him in this Mid-evil pocket universe of all places, but he was beginning to question the captain of the Queen Bohemia's sanity.

All that seemed to go on here was baking—baked rolls, baked cakes, baked pies, baked whatever could be baked. He was beginning to think his mind was becoming half-baked with all the baking. How long had it been since Bronson had dropped him off? Bronson had said he'd be back in five days, but he'd never said whether that was five Mid-evil days, five Earth days, or another measure of planetary rotation entirely. All Tobias knew was that days had been replaced by countless bags of flour, hot stoves, endless batches of rolls, and the watchful eye of the Master Baker, Arfustor. Or rather, watchful eyes, plural.

Four eyeballs, two of which had spectacles over

their tops that made the irises and pupils look twice their size, each located on the end of protruding stalks that swayed back and forth and up and down, never blinking nor turning away from him. Tobias trusted Bronson, but why this place with this bizarre being? If he didn't get out of here soon and back to the Collective, he felt like his head would burst. Arfustor smelled of flour and yeast, and his off-white baggy pants and white tank top were partly covered in the stuff.

"So, young fella, yer ever made a loaf of bread before?" Arfustor asked him.

"No."

"And why the bloody hell not, hey?"

Tobias raised an eyebrow. Because so far, they'd only made rolls and not loaves? "Because I've never needed to. There are always shops to buy food, and I've never been big on eating bread."

Arfustor squinted at him as he took off his spectacles and used a corner of his apron to wipe the lenses. "Blimey, who the bloody hell doesn't eat bread? Yer universe is a bit of a queer one if I should say so. Wot about do-nuts?"

"Now we're talking."

"We not be talkin', we be bakin'. Come with me and learn yerself some bakin'." He replaced the spectacles over his eyes and pointed a thumb over his shoulder to the open doorway situated almost directly opposite the stone bakery's main entrance.

Was this supposed to be part of the plan? Tobias didn't think so, but then on such a desolate-looking planet, what else was he going to do to spend his time? He begrudgingly followed Arfustor through the doorway, the warmth of a wood-fire stove hitting him like a brick wall. But it wasn't just the heat that hit him, it was the aroma of freshly brewed coffee beans and cooling bread. "Thank the gods, you have coffee here on your planet."

Arfustor turned on the spot and stared straight at him, each eyeball stilled. "And why in hell would we not 'ave coffee 'ere then, hey? You think we be some sorta primitive cave-dwelli' beasts in space?"

Tobias chose not to answer. This being seemed rather edgy. Hopefully, he wouldn't be stuck alone with the baker too long. It wasn't that he worried about his safety but the awkward silences. Arfustor's entire focus was on baking, which didn't leave them much in common to talk about. And less talking left more room for thinking than Tobias was comfortable with. Had he actually died? Was this place some kind of waypoint where he was meant to reflect on the decisions he'd made through his life before he could move on to the next stage of existence? If so, he was done with it. He missed having long, flowing conversations with like-minded people about the serious issues of the galaxy, although he often made sure the conversations were with the types not about to turn him in for ransom to his wife. Frell, how did the galaxy become so complicated?

The truth was, it had always been that way.

Arfustor grabbed the boiling kettle from the stove and motioned at two ceramic cups nearby. "Sugar?"

Tobias shook his head and put on an accent like Arfustor's. "Nah, mate, I'm sweet enough."

Arfustor's eyestalks stopped still again. "You takin' the piss?"

Tobias had no idea what Arfustor meant. "No, was just being silly. Never mind."

Arfustor turned away and grunted. About half a minute later, he handed Tobias a cup of black coffee. "Get that in yer. We've got a busy production ahead of us."

"Thanks." Tobias raised the cup, pretending not to notice the chip in the rim, and took a sip. As the flavors ran over his tongue and slid down his throat, he couldn't help but wonder if that was the most delicious coffee he had ever tasted. "Damn, this is great."

Arfustor placed his cup on the counter and put his hands on his hips. "Of course, it is. I source only the greatest beans on the planet. Aye, they cost me a pretty penny, but good coffee is worth it, hey?"

Tobias nodded. "So… what are we making today anyway?"

Arfustor smiled, and his eye-stalks moved as if performing some type of rhythmic dance. "Do-nuts. Lots of do-nuts. The local joustin' club is puttin' on an afternoon tea, celebrating twenty years. If yer 'ere long enough, I'll ask you along. Yer like joustin'?"

Was he hearing the baker right? Jousting? "I have never seen jousting before," and he resisted the urge to add the words, 'whatever that is,' at the end.

"Er, shame that. You'd 'ave a smashin' time too. Men dressed in shiny armor trying to knock each other off their horses. And lots of pretty ladies in their dresses." Arfustor shook his head. "Nah, our ladies be not to yer liking anyway." He turned around and opened a drawer beneath a bench covered in flour. He pulled out an apron and tossed it at Tobias. "Put this on, aye. Keeps the flour and stuff off yer clothes."

Tobias caught the protective garment and tied the straps of it behind his back. It didn't have a neck loop to hang over his head, unlike the ones he usually saw chefs wear at the restaurants he frequented. "I might need to point out again that I don't like to cook."

Arfustor's eye-stalks froze in place, and he crossed his arms. "Be ye flamin' serious? Wot kind of man don't like to cook?"

He watched the alien baker walk over to a pantry built into the wall, gather metal tins of various ingredients, and place them on the workbench. "I was born into privilege and married into even higher privilege," Tobias said.

Arfustor pulled a rolling pin out from a drawer and passed it to Tobias. "Yer need this, yer posh bugger." He made his way to a crate, pulled out a couple of logs, and threw them into the bottom part of the wood-burning stove. "We gonna need a flamin' hot stove fer fryin' these nuts. And I don't mean those little ones between yer legs."

Tobias chuckled. "Who said anything about small?"

The baker pointed at him. "Anyone who can wear tight pants like that can't be havin' much meat in their trousers." He grabbed another rolling pin from the same drawer where Tobias's came from. Arfustor grinned as he patted the wooden utensil against his palm. "This be me favorite pin. I call it The Crusher."

This guy seemed a little too excited about baking, but then, it was his occupation, his livelihood, and what he prided himself on, or at least that was what Tobias could derive from their brief time spent together. Thoughts swam through his mind as he fished for a conversation starter. "So why baking?"

"Do wot?" Arfustor asked. "Yer mean why do I bake? Well, that'd be because I want to." He pushed a set of metal scales along the bench, bringing it to a stop between them. "This first batch, until you get the hang of it, we be makin' just a two-pound dough."

Pounds? Tobias thought. He took a look around the place and didn't spot any machines. Were they about to do everything by hand?

The baker placed a metal bowl on top of the scale plate and fiddled around with the pile of metal weights until he found the ones he was after. "Two pounds of flour."

Tobias watched in fascination as the man's hands moved quicker than someone cheating in a card game as he poured flour into the metal bowl until he had the correct weight. This process continued as he added a few more ingredients. He held a packet for Tobias to see. "Now, without these fellas 'ere, the do-nuts aren't gonna be no good." He used a pair of scissors to cut a corner off the packet. "Don't yer be tellin' the locals I gots me these things. They'd be none too 'appy."

"They're just scissors." Tobias frowned but then thought that maybe Bronson had brought them on a previous visit. "Oh…"

"Aye. That's right. Yer not to be seein' no locals anyway." He began to pour the dry yeast into the bowl. "These yeast fellas, yer be best to make sure you get the weight perfect. Yer put the wrong amount of yeast in this, all sorts of crazy shit be happenin', and the wee buggers be scarce as golden eggs in these parts these days. So don't be wastin' 'em."

"Oh. Really?"

Arfustor grinned, and his eyes moved frantically on their stalks again. "Aye. Yer don't put the right amount in, yer could cause a rip in the space-time-continue-thingy."

"But it's just..."

"Ha! Gotcha. Nah, they can sink if not enough or grow blister blobs if yer put too much in. One batch I made, when I'd been at the rubbery dub too long, they looked like some poor bugger who caught the pox."

"Rubbery dub?"

"Pub. Do yer know any bloody thing?" Arfustor pulled the bowl off the scales and placed it on the counter. "Now, mind this next bit, aye? It be proper important."

This being spoke in a way Tobias had never heard, and he had seen much around the galaxy. But he made sure to watch what Arfustor did next.

"A bit of shoulder space, if yer don't mind." Arfustor lifted his elbows to convey his words.

"Of course." Tobias took a couple of steps to his left and watched the baker pull open a drawer and pull out a wooden spoon.

"I need some milk. See that cupboard next to yer? Grab one of the cups. Any cup will do. I call it a little somethin' I prepared earlier."

Tobias did as asked and noticed it was half full of something that looked like milk but with a tinge of yellow. He didn't dare sniff it nor ask exactly what type of milk it was. "'Ere yer go, fella," Tobias tried to emulate Arfustor's way of speaking.

Arfustor's eyestalks ceased movement. "Think yer funny, do yer?"

Tobias straightened his expression. He sure as hell didn't mean to upset this being, who he thought could be quite dangerous in a fight. "Um..."

The baker threw his head back and placed a hand on his stomach as he burst out laughing. "Bugger me. Yer should've seen yer face. Okay, now pour that milk into this bowl nice an' slow. Keep it straight as if yer pissin' on a silver piece."

Tobias did as asked, and while pouring the peculiar-looking 'milk,' the baker rapidly spun the bowl in a clockwise direction while mixing the ingredients with the wooden spoon with the other hand. It was a sight to behold, the alien baker working as if he was a mixing machine. He kept pouring the liquid at the same, consistent speed until he drained it completely.

"Yer did good," Arfustor said and continued to mix the ingredients, slowly forming a crème-colored dough.

"Bet you wish you had four arms like a Monsatan."

"Do wot? I 'ave never heard of such a thing, but I

'ave yet to leave this planet."

"Would you like to?"

"No bleedin' way. A feller should be content with wot he 'as... a home, a job, and a drinkin' hole not far. All I need is a lady-friend. I'm not fussy as long as she has the right stuff. Know wot I mean?"

"Yes, I do." Yes, he could sure tell this baker a story or two.

"Yer married?" Arfustor's mixing speed hadn't slowed at all.

"Technically, yes." He frowned. "Didn't Bronson tell you why I'm here?"

"Nah, and I didn't care to ask. 'Twas quite the queer night when I first met the cheeky bugger. Yer know, fer the flamin' life of me, I still couldn't say how he found me, but he did. Every now and then, he calls in, asks me fer a favor, and gives me some brilliant bakin' equipment."

It sounded like the pair had a mutually beneficial arrangement. The baker's hands continued to work as if their owner had injected himself with some kind of caffeine or snorted a speed-enhancing drug, all without raising a sweat. A few moments passed, and Arfustor declared the mixing was done.

"Thanks fer yer steady hands, fella. Now we let this rest fer a wee while, let the yeast do its thing." He placed a damp cloth over the bowl.

"Rest? Didn't you say you had a deadline?"

"Aye, of course, but patience is the key. Yer can't

just rush like a bull at a gate with these things."

"How many will this batch make?"

"About two dozen and three."

"And how many do you need to make for the jousting competition?"

"One hundred."

"Frell. That means..."

"Yep, three more batches. We 'ave time, I've measured it exactly. We don't wanna 'ave 'em all made too early, and each batch needs rest. Good donuts need care."

Tobias didn't like the idea of being stuck at Arfustor's all day baking. Again. If Bronson were to appear within the next moment, he'd be only too happy to run off back in his ship.

"Fella, yer seem to be thinkin' some. Not everything in life should be rushed. The secret to good bakin' is like pleasin' the ladies. Take yer time and treat a lady right, and she'll be the tastiest treat yer ever ate." Arfustor waggled his eye-stalks suggestively and grinned.

Tobias stared at the baker. Not sure if he should laugh or not. That was a weird analogy to make. They didn't really eat women on this planet, did they? Or was Arfustor making the euphemism that Tobias thought he was?

"Wot?" Arfustor's smile slipped. "Don't tell me yer never known a good woman? You said yer was married."

Tobias looked at the cloth-covered bowl. "My wife is...." He let the sentence trail off, unsure how to describe Rosamunde Cruz in a way this baker could understand and coming up empty, so he tried again. "My wife is... well, I'm supposed to be dead, but for how long, I have no idea. We switched a clone to take my place so my wife could interrogate me. She has torture techniques that you wouldn't believe. So I guess by hiding here, she has no way of finding me."

"Yer wife? Wot kind of marriage is that, exactly?"

"Rose and I were an arranged marriage. It's quite common where I'm from."

Arfustor lifted a section of cloth from the bowl and took a peek. "Ha! Not ready yet. So yer mean to tell me that someone tells yer who yer 'ave to marry? Struth, sounds like the royal family 'ere."

"Royal family?"

Arfustor's eyestalks darted around. "Aye, come see over 'ere." He guided Tobias to a window located near his storage pantry. "See that over yonder?" He pointed. "That's one of the turrets of the castle where they live. Never met a royal meself, but they say if yer can sell yer goods to 'em, yer made it. One day, mate, one day."

A royal family in these parts? He had so many questions he could ask.

"Aye, so tell me a little more about yer marriage."

Tobias sighed. He hardly knew this man, but he

felt as though sharing his story would be okay. The baker had no gain to turn him in nor desire. "I come from a political family with merchant ties stretching back many generations. We did well, but as is often the case in many influential families, it was all about politics when it came to marriage. My mother suggested that if I were to marry someone with ties to the Trade Corporation, it would benefit the family greatly and secure our future. It made sense, and one night at a Trade Corporation fundraiser dinner, I was introduced to Rosamunde Cruz. She was beautiful, of course. Green eyes that saw right through you, a face you would want to wake up to every morning, and the body of a Miss Galaxy winner."

Arfustor's eyes froze. "I 'ave no idea wot yer talkin' about, but keep at it."

"She could have any man she wanted at any time. Turned out that night she wanted me, so we snuck off to a hotel room where the function was located and... discovered we were compatible. At least we were that night."

"You two did the whole shaggin' thing on the night yer met? That's just wrong."

"In hindsight, it was. She disappeared sometime before I woke. I never saw her again for three months, at which time she told me she was pregnant with my baby, and the match had met approval. I think at that time, I already knew it was a mistake, but the baby she was carrying is one of my favorite mistakes."

Arfustor didn't respond.

"So then…"

"Okie dokie, that dough should be ready now." Arfustor grabbed a handful of flour from a tin and gently dusted the workbench, leaving a thin covering. "This is the fun bit." He tipped the bowl over and caressed the lump of dough. "Aye, that feels lovely. Get yer paws on that."

Tobias shrugged, but as he felt the dough, he marveled at the workmanship that went into making it. "Nice."

"Glad yer like it. Now get rollin' while I ready the next batch, hey?"

"Um, sure." Tobias grabbed the rolling pin and did as asked while the Master Baker weighed up the ingredients for the next dough.

"Keep rollin'. Yer want it to be about a fingernail thick."

Tobias soon found that his lack of manual labor during his life got the better of him. However, he did as asked, and a thumbs up from the machine that was Arfustor put a smile on his face. "I'm going to need a nice cold pint once we're done."

"Yer keep workin' like that, I'll make sure yer get one."

Arfustor grabbed two cutters from a drawer beneath the bench and used the larger one to make a number of large circles and then the smaller ones to make a round hole inside them. He put the do-nuts to one side, grabbed what was left of the dough, and molded it into a ball. He asked Tobias to roll it out again and use the cutters to make more do-nuts while he began to weigh up a third batch of dough. The process of switching jobs between each other took a couple of hours, and they soon had a bench full of do-nuts ready for frying.

"No offense to yer, mate, but I'd best be doin' this 'ere bit. So wot happened next, hey?"

Tobias raised an eyebrow. "You mean with my marriage?"

"Aye. Of course, ya daft bugger."

"Rose and I never found that flame again, like the one that caused my girl Ellie to exist. Sure, we had some sex, and it wasn't all bad, but it didn't take long for her to get bored, so I was told. She had her favorite men, and I don't think she even tried to keep it a secret, and then one day I fell into temptation myself. On a diplomatic mission to Endaria, I was invited to a post-function celebration. Apparently, the five moons of Endaria can only be seen by night once every four cycles. There was a feast and plenty of drink to be had on the banks of the Great Endar Lake. There were plenty of people around, and after a while, the Endarians disappeared. It was getting very late in the night, and just me and five human men were partaking. But then the Endarians returned, and the previously unseen women came out of the nearby palace, wrapped only in thin robes. If there's a more beautiful creature than an Endarian, I've yet to meet one."

"More beautiful than Bubbles?" Arfustor dropped a couple of do-nuts into a pan of fat, making a swish as the liquid cooked the dough.

"Bubbles? The Travanian in Bronson's crew?" Tobias couldn't see the attraction.

"Well, of course, 'er. Wot's wrong with yer? Thick, strong thighs and that massive head. Cor… she's a tasty treat that one." Arfustor made a motion with his hands that suggested he enjoyed the size of the Travanian woman's assets.

"It's all about personal taste, I guess. So these women, I don't know how many there were, nor how many men followed them out of the palace, walked over to the lake and dropped their robes. One, in particular, caught my eye, and I must have caught hers. She winked at me and signaled me to come over. As I got near, I nearly fainted at the perfection of her completely naked form, and she told me I needed to remove my clothes if I was to join her for a swim.

"Geezus! I nearly burnt one of me do-nuts." Arfustor fussed about and continued to fry them. "So you and 'er, yer did it?"

One way to cut the story short. "After a few hours

swimming, yes, we gave into the temptations of each other's flesh. And that was how my second daughter, Caree, came into the world."

"Wow. Yer sure get 'round, hey? Yer still putting babies in ladies bellies as soon as yer meet 'em?"

Tobias chuckled, but as his mind went to Caree's mother, Terese, he became tense. "I'm more content trying to bring people together to bring Rose down. It's sad. When we first met, I'd never have guessed she was capable of the things she's done. But I was much younger, naïve, and just a politically motivated transport captain in my family's merchant business."

"So wot about the other woman then?"

A lump rose in Tobias's throat. "She was murdered. The records will say it was a pirate attack, but I know Rose was behind it. But I can't prove it, ever."

"Well, fuck me. That's just rubbish."

The two worked in silence, but they had produced one hundred and eight golden do-nuts after another hour. Tobias stood back from the racks of cooling do-nuts and surveyed their handiwork with a sense of pride. "Wow, so we're all done now?"

Arfustor laughed out loud. "Now we 'ave to frost 'em." He looked at Tobias's facial reaction to the news of yet more work to complete. "The frosting is wot makes 'em come back fer more, if yer know wot

I mean?"

Tobias grinned at Arfustor's wink and nudge. "Okay, let's do this then."

The baker made his way back to the pantry and pulled out a selection of glass bottles. "Now, it's best yer not tell anyone about some of this, hey? But I have some of the best flavors and colors among these bottles 'ere as well as some other secret ingredients."

"Secret ingredients?" Tobias rubbed his beard.

"Well, let's just say me do-nuts can 'ave an effect on women if I were to use a particular bottle 'ere. I usually let me baking do the talkin'. Yer know, a woman loves a man who can bake something yummy fer 'em. Yer make 'em a good cake or tasty dessert, she's as good as yours. But Bubbles, well, I 'ave been tempted to splash some of this 'ere concoction in a special do-nut fer 'er, but it wouldn't be right."

Tobias stared at the glass vial filled with a dark liquid that Arfustor pointed at. It had a cork stopper and a paper label that was peeling off on one side. The contents were written in faded ink and hard to make out. It could've said vanilla. But it could have been a bunch of flourished hearts as well. "Are you telling me you have a love potion that will get a woman to fall for you?"

Arfustor placed the tray on the workbench and crossed his arms. "Aye, it might do. Or it might make 'em spill the beans as it were. But I 'ave yet to use it, and I don't think I will. But if I was to turns me back, someone could possibly use it. Yer know, fer a batch of frostin' fer those few extra do-nuts, they could do wot needs to be done. But best be careful, there be no tellin' wot that potion could do in yer galaxy. Could even be fatal. I'm very careful wot I put in the frosting fer Bronson and his lot."

Of course! He could try it, as foolish as it sounded in his head, but he knew Rose had a weakness for exotic foods.

"Yes, maybe they could." He reached for the vial as Arfustor busied himself mixing up some frosting.

15

Phoenix saw.

Phoenix felt.

Phoenix thought.

He recognized the cold presence of thousands of beings desiring his raw energy. Like leeches, they came up to him, two or three at a time trying to latch on. But he used his mind to push them away, even with his stunted size. He was able to protect his mother and everyone and keep them safe. Her arms were about him as she walked and kept his eyes closed as he fed on her breast.

What was with this body he was given? So small, and he was always hungry. The milk did nothing for him but make him want to pee all the time. He needed something more filling, the energy balls that constantly whispered to him but remained out of his reach. He called to them and they to him. He needed them to give him their energy, but he needed his mind back to where he was now, not thinking about food. He needed lots of things.

"Phoenix, slow down. You'll hurt yourself."

His mother was worried, her voice filled with concern, but she was wrong. He didn't need to slow down, he needed to speed up to grow faster. He was already so much stronger than when he'd first been born on Amasis and capable of doing things now he couldn't back then when he'd been a newborn infant. But he needed more power to protect them all. He was part biological, part mimetic energy trapped in a tiny humanoid body that hindered his ability. Even with his eyes closed, he could see the bio-signatures of the beings his mother wanted so desperately to reach. They were nearby but were cut off from them by the presence of the parasites that infected the planet. They were filling her head with illusions about where she was, telling her not to move and forcing her to stop, their pleasure from her fear and frustration was nauseating. There were thousands of them, so many that Phoenix couldn't see them all. These invisible entities wanted to imprison them all and especially him, so they could feed endlessly on all the hallucinations they created. The shifters were fighting them but couldn't win. There wasn't enough energy to replenish them as they weakened. Phoenix saw that too.

Their parasitic hunger bit at him with their need

to consume him. But his mother's arms were around him, and he felt that most of all—her love and her strength.

Tiredness threatened to overcome Phoenix, frustrating him as he had work to do to save this planet from the relentless hunger that sought to destroy all life on it. The mind-eaters wanted to use him, but they weren't knowledgeable of his full capabilities.

His mother stumbled and nearly fell. She was blind to her surroundings. Phoenix couldn't stop the illusion this time—he was weak, and there were just too many. If only he were bigger and stronger. The mind-eaters surrounded them, filling his mother with paralyzing fear. One of the creatures attempted to dig into his mind with its claw-like thoughts. He could stop it, but as the shadowy creature started to draw from his dwindling energy reserves, he could see its thoughts and realized its weakness.

Like a cold, clammy hand, the creature reached inside him and seized a small orb of pure energy from him. He let the parasite take the energy.

The mind eater rejoiced.

This is what it wanted.

A new source of energy that it could feed off of forever. Surely, a child like him could live forever, couldn't it? He was special, unique, capable of giving them life and destroying everything. The mind eater ingested the energy, too hungry to see the warnings it should've seen.

Phoenix focused his attention and used the link created by the mind-eater's feeding to create a massive power surge. Like a bomb going off, the mind eater exploded in a satisfying spray of energy that Phoenix consumed as it touched him. Seeming oblivious to their brethren's demise, a few more mind-eaters gained access to his mind, feeding on what they desired, not seeing the fatal consequences of their actions.

"Phoenix!" he heard his mother yell as if from far away. "Stop, you're going to get hurt."

He ignored the warning, allowing more of the energy suckers in, none of them realizing the error of their ways until it was too late. Even as he absorbed the energy created from their deaths, he grew tired, his small body needing more rest than what he had time to give it.

"Help us!" he heard his mother scream.

His eyes remained closed. Hands grabbed onto him, lifting him from the protection of her arms and carrying him away from her.

No, not now.

NOT NOW!

He had to save the others and this planet.

Desperate to finish what he'd started, he left off a few more mind bombs in what he hoped was a chain reaction. But the darkness was too quick, and he could no longer see the world around him. And his mother's arms were no longer holding nor protecting him. And all he could hear was the silence of unconsciousness.

Ellie lay in the cage, deep in sleep. They had come for her again, but this time the dreams weren't as scary.

She walked in a field, the type that she had seen many times as a teenager on Endaria, flowers of all colors growing. She heard that these types of gardens used to grow on Earth, long before she was born. It was the eve of her sixteenth birthday, the white summer dress flowed past her knees, and the lush growth rubbed gently against her bare feet with each step she took.

"Ellie!" a male voice called out.

She spun around, hoping to see Axel, but she doubted he'd have traveled to these parts. Darius Cruz looked her up and down. "You look beautiful." He walked close to her.

"What is it you want?" she snapped. She'd never liked her cousin that much. He was always getting her in trouble with her mother.

"I'm so bored on this planet. Everyone is so vanilla."

Darius had been into wild parties ever since he turned thirteen, and with his connections, nothing was off-limits to him—prostitutes of both genders and various species, drugs and stimulants, alcohol so potent that few Travanians even dared to drink it. "No, Darius."

"Oh, come on, help me find a fast ship, so we can go off and party and be back before any of our parents realize we're gone."

Ellie looked at him, his eyes pleading for her to take him somewhere. She knew of a spaceport nearby where she could drop him off and come back and say she knew nothing about where he went. She stared through him into the endless gardens as if something about this moment had happened before. "Okay, let's go," she said.

The pair sprinted from the gardens to an outdoor hangar field where many Trade Corporation ships were docked. She spotted one perfect for what they needed.

"Ellie, where do you think you're going?" a male human called out.

Ellie spun and looked at the man, one of her mother's many lovers. Or was it? This one was blue like an Endarian but human and also something else. Recognition sparked.

"Phoenix?" Ellie whispered.

How could this be?

He was just a baby.

Not a grown man.

"We are," Phoenix said as he disappeared into a wisp of blue smoke. Ellie reached for him, but her hand passed through emptiness. "Phoenix!"

Ellie sat up in her cage and looked around.

"Are you okay?" Axel asked.

Ellie nodded. "Yes, I think something's changed. I saw Phoenix."

"Something's changed," Hendrix said.

The shifters who had been lost in battle and had risen to fight against their brethren as the undead were once again falling to the ground, only this time they weren't rising. Seeing them fall was like watching a wind blow through the field that knocked them over as it touched them.

Had their reanimation been an illusion to begin with? Were the mind-eaters losing power?

Hendrix fervently hoped so. "Spread out, the masses are thinning. Let's crush them!"

"Why don't we leave the rest and just grab what we need from here and take the ship?" Zodial, one of the three surviving fighters in his group, asked.

"Gothani has secured enough Stardrives by now, for sure."

"And leave this planet to go to hell with the solids still on it?" Hendrix shook his head. "We work together, them and us. None of you would've been freed if it wasn't for them."

The shifter snarled, but the four continued the battle, slaying enemy after enemy as they swung their weapons around. The mind-eaters did seem to be losing numbers and not regaining any. Hendrix allowed himself to smile—soon he'd have everything he needed to start a new life.

Phoenix opened his eyes. His mother was lying beside him on the floor, but he felt something pushing into his arms. Stardrives. He was in a room with Stardrives, and three of them hovered above him, their tentacles touching his arms. Their warmth was incredible, their strength renewing. Their whispered words of comfort were soothing.

"They're feeding you energy and nutrients. We were worried you had gotten badly hurt." Caree stroked his cheek with her fingers.

He looked into her eyes. So much love for him, not only in the way she looked at him but in how their energies communicated with each other's showed more love than any normal senses could convey. "I need to keep fighting," he said to her.

Caree nodded. He didn't need to say it out loud, she knew, and he knew that she knew she couldn't stop him. Bolstered by the presence of the Stardrives, he closed his eyes again and invited the parasites to enter his mind. He knew their secret now. How they were connected, and he was ready to use his mind bombs against them again. The density of the mind-eater presence was increasing.

'*Child.*' The mind-eater hoard hissed at him in his mind. '*You will submit.*'

The energy-sucking vampire-type creatures were strong, crowding around him, fighting to overwhelm him with their collective presence. They were drawn to him from all across the planet now, focusing their energy in an attempt to force him to surrender and become what they wanted, what they'd tried to make the Stardrives become and failed in their insatiable greed. How were they able to get to Amasis in the first place? His thoughts were filled with their whispered answers as he witnessed through their memories their ascension to power and their intentions to take over more worlds.

"I won't allow it," he said out loud and drew a long steady breath. Inside his mind, he focused his thoughts and created the largest mind bomb he could, drawing on energy from the trio of Stardrives connected to him as well as his mother. The energy filled him like a roar that vibrated his very cells, wanting to be unleashed.

"You won't win," he said when he could endure no more and let the power loose.

16

The wave of energy hit Hendrix like a massive gust of wind, strong enough to lift him and the others around him off their feet and throw them to the ground. He clutched at his head and closed his eyes, trying to block the sound of screaming, aware it might be his own voice echoing inside his mind. Or maybe the shriek of thousands of enraged mind-eaters desperate to survive. Or the scream of a child whose rage could destroy an entire planet. Or maybe it was a mixture of all three.

The screaming ended as suddenly as it began, as did the mind-splitting blast of mental energy. Hendrix blinked and looked around. The sudden lack of pressure on his mind was as deafening as was the unexpected sense of relief it provided, and the world around him was gone. No, not gone precisely, more that the illusion created by the mind-eaters was gone. The parasites had clearly affected them more than he'd thought. Gone was the vast plain of gray clay shrouded in darkness. In its place, pale sunlight shone through wisps of smoke, which curled in tendrils from the cracked and broken ground. Deep fissures marred the surface, splitting the battlefield with uneven crags and jagged rocks strewn about as if tossed by an angry god. Or a dying planet. As if in answer to that thought, the ground trembled beneath Hendrix's half-prone body. He slowly got to his feet, shielding his eyes from the sudden change in brightness, and glanced around at the others who were doing the same.

"What the frell just happened?" one of the nearest shifters asked.

"I think Phoenix happened." The taste of the child's energy was undeniable, slightly bitter, and far too powerful.

"That baby did this?"

"Not the damage to the planet, no, but the mind-eaters..." He shook his head, a mixture of fear and admiration tightening his spine. "He killed the mind-eaters." What kind of power did Phoenix possess that he could do something like that? But the results were undeniable. The mind-eaters were nowhere to be seen or felt. All that remained were what was left of their bodies strewn across the plain, the ones that had fallen in hand-to-hand combat, at least. The thousands of others that had been killed in the psychic blast had simply vanished. Did that mean they were dead or had they been banished to a different place? There was no way to tell. But Hendrix had been right in being concerned about how fast Phoenix was growing. If he could do something like this during infancy, what was he capable of as an adult? And what did it mean for them?

"That's no baby," one of the shifters said as if sharing Hendrix's thoughts.

The ground rumbled beneath their feet, making it difficult to stand. Hendrix put his arms out to his sides, struggling to remain balanced. Such a strong quake in the face of so much structural damage was never a good sign.

"We need to leave," he said to the others. "This planet is falling apart. Gothani?" he called into his wrist comm. He sensed her presence, so he knew she was alive, but what of the Stardrives and the ship?

"Hendrix. Did you feel that blast?" she asked without hesitation.

"We more than felt it. The mind-eaters are gone."

"Here too. The child set off some kind of psychic bomb that ripped through everything and knocked us out for a moment. I'm on the cargo ship with him and his mother. They're both out cold. Bronson and the other two from the Bohemia are waking."

"What of the Stardrives?"

"Two of the ones we rescued sacrificed themselves and gave their power to the child, and a third was damaged in the process. I doubt it will make it. But we have several dozen onboard, including their vines, that are in good condition and should last the trip to wherever we take them for resettlement. Enough, maybe, to start a new colony of them. But I don't think they'll willingly go anywhere without the child. They are crowding around him and his mother right now. I'm not sure if they're protecting him or vice versa at this point."

"That could be a problem," Hendrix said. They needed Stardrives to survive. But what if the bio-mimetic life forms wouldn't allow them access unless Phoenix gave it? A so-called child of such power could easily destroy their future. The ground heaved beneath his feet, slamming him to his knees. The tremor subsided, but the rumbling deep below the surface continued like a warning growl. "We'll have to figure it out later," he called into his comm. "This planet is—"

"Falling apart, yes, I'm aware," Gothani said. "The Travanian's readings indicate the rate of destabilization is increasing exponentially. We need to leave before it loses complete cohesion."

"Agreed. I'm sending everyone to you now. The ship is flight-ready?"

"It's old, but yes."

"Good. Prepare to launch but wait for the others.

I'm heading to the Bohemia and will rendezvous with you later."

"The Bohemia? Why?"

"I'm not leaving without our collateral. I have the feeling we'll need Thalia as a bargaining chip when the rest of the galaxy realizes that seventy-odd shifters are alive and well."

"Ah, the Collective will want her for sure. She must have all of Rosamunde Cruz's secrets stored in her memory. Hendrix, I was wrong about you. You're a worthy leader."

Hendrix didn't bother replying and cut the comm signal instead. Would she think so later when she realized what his plan was? He doubted it. She'd probably think he was as reckless as he felt and a traitor, but great risk was never without great reward if it paid off. Of course, it was always the gamble.

He sent a message to all the remaining shifters to head to the cargo vessel in the hangar and turned to the four nearest him, the four he'd been fighting beside for the last several hours and knew he could count on to have his back and get the job done as required.

"It's time," was all he said and headed for the Bohemia, his chosen crew falling into line beside him.

Caree sat straight up from where she'd been lying on the floor. She placed a hand on her chest to steady her thundering heartbeat and tried to focus on her surroundings through her blurred vision. She was inside some kind of ship's cargo hold, but everything was unfamiliar—the walls, the flooring, the soft blankets that someone had piled around her and Phoenix.

"Phoenix!" He was huddled in a ball within the blankets, several dimly lit Stardrives hovering nearby. She screamed his name again, but he didn't move. A wave of panic, grief, and anger crashed through her. "No..." She reached for him and pulled him flat on his back. She pressed her ear to his chest. He had a pulse so that was something. With his eyes shut and chest gently rising and falling, he appeared to be at peace. "What have you done?" she asked her son, but the unnerving silence remained as his answer. Her head still pounded from the force of the blast he'd let loose.

The floor shook beneath her. She crouched over Phoenix, protecting him, as the metal beneath the blankets vibrated with a low groan.

"What the frell?" she called out as the trembling subsided after a minute. Caree put a hand up to shield her eyes from dust falling from above her head. The murkiness of her thoughts made it hard to think. She'd lost track of where she was on this strange planet. The last thing she remembered was trying to find Ellie and Axel, but every corner she'd turned had led her back to the transport hangar with Bronson, Marsais, and Bubbles just as confused as she'd been. It was as if the grays had done something to her head. Or maybe it hadn't been the grays but something else. Then Phoenix had fought off some kind of mental attack that had left him exhausted. And then the next thing she knew, she was in the ship with Gothani and the others, and there were many Stardrives. She glanced around at the room filled with the dim glow of several clusters of the orbs. She'd never seen so many in one place before, and one had its tendrils lightly touching Phoenix. He smiled but didn't wake.

Sleep. The thought whispered in her mind like a soft breeze filled with sunlight. *Heal.* It was more an impression than a word.

"That's right, you helped him. But what about the others?"

Protect.

"In here," a voice called out from the corridor that led past the open door to the room. "I think she's awake."

"Gothani?" Caree called out as loudly as her

spinning mind allowed. Shifters. She sensed them now too. How many were left after the fight? As much as the shifters' presence disrupted her empathic state, she worried they would be lost in the war against the mind-eaters. Those formless creatures were the most dangerous beings she had ever encountered.

"It's okay, Caree," Gothani said, entering the room followed by Bronson. The shifter seemed to be flickering as if holding her shape was difficult. Caree remembered it happening earlier when the shifters had fed in the Stardrive grove but not to the same extent. As if sensing her question, Gothani gestured at the many Stardrives that occupied the room. "Our bodies naturally respond to their energy. I'm not used to being around so many."

The room shook again, only a few seconds before a deafening rumble filled her ears. A glance showed Phoenix still blissfully asleep, the Stardrives hovering closer.

"My ba…" she started.

"We've got him," another female voice said as Marsais appeared beside her. She gently stroked Phoenix's cheek, a soft smile curving her cat-like lips. "He saved everyone. He killed all the mind-eaters."

Everyone. The word echoed in Caree's mind. There was something else she needed to do here. Someone else who needed her. Ellie, Kendrick, Axel, the others? Were they alive? The connection she shared with her half-sister wasn't dead. Ellie, at least, was still alive and somewhere not far away. She needed to get to her and get them all to safety.

"The Stardrives won't let us move Phoenix to sick bay," Marsais said to Bronson. "They want him here."

"They're healing him." Caree smiled at the group of energy globes hovering above them, sharing their warm glow. "He needs their energy." He needed them now more than he needed her at the moment.

"Stay with them here then, while I look for the others," Bronson said.

"No..." Caree shook her head. She pushed against the ground and slowly rose to her feet. "To find the others, you'll need me."

"She's right," Gothani agreed. "She can sense things better than anyone except that baby, and we don't have time to go hunting."

"The scanners are frelled," Bubbles added. She shook her head and frowned at the holographic directional display from her wrist comm which appeared to be more static than anything else. "There's too much dimensional distortion now."

"I'm not leaving my sister and the others behind again," Caree said, facing Bronson.

"Okay, but we need to move fast. You look a little groggy." Bronson gave her a once over, frowning.

"I'll be okay."

Her strength grew with each passing moment, but the process felt accelerated compared to her normal recovery time, of course.

Phoenix. The Stardrives. They were sharing their energy, renewing her focus and clarity. She needed to hurry. All their lives hung in the balance.

"Take care of my baby," she said to Marsais and the Stardrives. She'd never been apart from him before, but he was safer here than going with her. And if anything happened to her and she didn't make it back, the Stardrives would continue to protect Phoenix. He was partly their child too. She needed to remember that.

If a newborn baby possessed power as strong as he did, what would he grow into? And to think he could also pass such energy to her while unconscious, her mind boggled. *May he never be corrupted by any evil,* she thought. As long as she was near, she vowed it would never happen.

"Let's go," she said to Bronson. "We don't have much time left."

Axel fell to his back as the ground lifted beneath his feet and jutted at a near right-angle. Was this actually happening? "Did you feel that?" he asked Ellie.

"Of course, I felt that. Everyone did. It's an aftershock from some big quake that happened. The fourth we've had in the past five minutes," Ellie snapped. She stood above him, reaching out to assist him to his feet.

"Not the quake," Axel said. "The other thing. It felt like a bomb went off in my head."

"Oh, that. Yeah. I thought I must have hit my head or something when I fell, but it looks like whatever happened wrecked the planet."

Axel glanced around. The cell they'd been in was gone. The walls were demolished and turned to rubble. Some of the damage appeared fresh, while other parts could've been weeks or even months old. The floor was split open, revealing fissures in the rock beneath that spewed tendrils of smoke which filtered the daylight into a haze. There was no sign of their captors, the mind-eaters and the ever-present pressure of their control were gone, and the sense of relief and confusion was tremendous. Was this another illusion?

"Is everyone okay?" he asked. He kept his hold on Ellie's hand while he checked for the others. Kendrick, Shiznit, and Uncle Henry were covered in dust and tiny bits of debris but accounted for.

"We must use haste. The planet is slipping away," Henry said. "To remain where we are could spell doom for us all. Everyone!"

Kendrick smirked. "Oh shit, Uncle Henry is crazier than before. I didn't think that was possible."

Shiznit used his skills at jumping to leap around the area surrounding them. "I can see a path."

"Yes, but none of us can jump like a spiced-up Miner Monkey like you," Kendrick said.

Shiznit raised an eyebrow. "A what?"

"It doesn't matter right now. Let the goat-man show us the way through. The planet will soon disappear, as well as all of us if we remain here." Henry blew into an open palm and raised his hand as if throwing something away.

"I think he hit his head a bit too hard," Ellie whispered to Axel.

"But what happened?" Axel asked. Everything was so different it was hard to take in. How long had they been captives on Amasis? What the hell was going on with all the quakes? And where had all the grays gone?

"I don't know," Ellie said. "Something blew up, and now we can escape. So let's not look a gift horse in the mouth, and get going." She tugged at his hand and started to make her way through the rubble.

Shiznit jogged and took the lead, his nimble legs navigating the least cumbersome way through the crumbling environment. Ellie and Axel followed closely behind Henry, and finally, Kendrick tagged along at the end of the group.

"This is so strange." Ellie bent to look at what had once been part of the railing of the broken corridor they were following. "Some of this damage has moss growing on it as if it happened years ago. But wasn't this place intact when we walked through it before? I don't remember there being any damage." She flicked at the dried chunk of moss with her finger. It fell past the railing to the ground. Ellie leaned forward to see where it had landed and let out a loud gasp. "Oh, frell."

Axel leaned past her to see what she was seeing and froze. A bony torso and skull jutted from beneath the section of the collapsed corridor they followed. Covered in debris and dust, it was hard to distinguish from the surroundings, but the size and shape of the skull were unmistakable as belonging to the grays. "They're dead."

"Long dead," Ellie agreed. She reached for Axel's hand again and gave it a tight squeeze.

"At least some of them are. These look pretty fresh over here," Kendrick added. He was on the other side of the corridor, looking at the mounds of fallen building materials that had collapsed during a recent quake. Limbs belonging to the Amasis guardians poked out from beneath the rubble. Arms, legs, all with flesh still intact and dried blood, were black against the gray dust.

"They were crushed trying to escape," Ellie said.

Axel stared at the remains. "At least we know they were really here and what happened to them, and we aren't completely losing our minds."

"How interesting." Uncle Henry bent and peered at the foot nearest him. "Tri-digitigrade toe webbing." He straightened again and looked at the others. "The owners of this planet have long vacated, I believe, knowing of the threat these mind-eaters pose. The few that were here were mostly illusions. The fact we couldn't tell the difference, my fellow travelers, clearly corroborates the uncertainty that the locals had in our abilities to defeat the enemy."

Axel frowned. "They left us behind to be convenient food... a distraction while they escaped just like Hendrix."

"But Caree came back," Ellie said. "The last dream, or whatever you wish to call it, ended abruptly. I saw Phoenix. Except he wasn't a baby anymore. Which means Hendrix came back too."

"How would you know? And why the sudden belief in Hendrix?" Axel asked. "You've never trusted him before."

"And I don't trust him now either." Ellie crossed her arms and stared at him. "But I trust my sister, and if she were here, she'd bring help. Someone or something kicked the mind-eaters' asses, right?"

"Yeah..." Axel agreed reluctantly. He hated when she made sense. "But that doesn't mean Hendrix did that or even came back with her if she did. It could've been something completely different."

Kendrick chuckled out loud, nearly stepping into a newly created hole in the ground in the process. He put out his hand to catch his balance and stop the others from following. "Ah... guys, all I see below this hole is blackness."

"We need to keep moving." Axel gestured toward the piles of rubble down the corridor that led to their eventual destination of the hangar. Or at least he hoped it did. There was no real way of telling if anything was where they remembered it being. Illusion was one thing, but it all could've collapsed during the earthquakes. "Keep an eye all around you for any holes in the floor. Who knows what's below all this?"

A thunderous crack ripped through the air. Axel made a hasty step backward followed by a glance, and the ground beneath his feet appeared to be shifting. "Frell. This whole place is moving." Or was it? Was his mind still playing tricks on him? The doubt gave him renewed sympathy for Uncle Henry who never seemed quite sure of where he was since being released from captivity in the Borbian prison. Add to that trauma the weeks spent enduring nightmarish illusions on Amasis, it was a wonder the old man still knew his name.

He turned to Shiznit in time to see the shins and feet of the Gho'bar disappear through the top of the corridor roof where it had collapsed into a pile of rubble. Shit, they would have to climb to get to the next section, which he couldn't even see. But Shiznit had never let him down, and he'd follow his trusty companion anywhere. "Hey, Shiz, slow down, buddy. Not all of us have goat feet."

Shiznit's head poked through the opening and peered back at them. "You wanted me to lead the way. So, I'm leading."

"You're just hungry," Axel replied with a grin. "You forgot to bring snacks again." When was the last time they'd properly eaten anything? They'd been provided with some kind of nourishment while imprisoned, or they'd all be dead by now, but even Kendrick's bulky frame seemed thin compared to when they'd arrived on the planet.

Axel's foot slipped as he climbed, the cracked stone from the wrecked surroundings sliding down as he did so. If he was having trouble navigating the precarious terrain, how would his uncle cope? "Are you okay, Uncle Henry?"

The old man grunted, navigating a section of rubble beside him. "Compared to some places where I've ventured, this is like an Endarian palace floor."

Axel nodded, relieved to see his uncle still had spirit left. He knew better than to ask Ellie, who could climb better than him, ever since—

"Axel!" a female voice called through the hole in

the ceiling. "Ellie!"

The voice sounded like Caree's.

"Yes, sister, we're down here!" Ellie called back. She turned to look at Axel, her eyes glittering with excitement. "Told you she was here. She'd never abandon me."

She bounded up the slope, not caring about the mini avalanches of pebble-sized proportions that cascaded in her wake and threatened to knock Axel off his feet.

"We need to hurry," Henry called out, following Ellie's lead. "Come on, son, stop slacking."

Kendrick grinned as he passed Axel, trailing Uncle Henry. "Yeah, son, stop slacking."

"Frell," Axel muttered beneath his breath as he scrambled to keep up with the others. Why exactly had he brought his brother along on this trip? The pain and muscle fatigue of being imprisoned was fast catching up to him as he reached the top of the pile of debris. He paused to catch his breath and looked directly up through the hole in the ceiling that Kendrick had helped Uncle Henry pass through. A sheet of metal jutted out from the side, missing his face by mere inches, but otherwise, the opening was fairly broad and not compromised. The distance wasn't far, only about a half-body length in height, but before he could lift himself, a familiar male face peered over the edge.

"Thought you guys could use a hand." The captain of the Queen Bohemia grinned as he offered Axel his outstretched palm.

"Bronson?" Axel paused. "What the frell are you doing here?" Not Hendrix then. Bronson had helped Caree come back for them. Not surprising, really. The crew of the Queen Bohemia always seemed to arrive just when someone needed them. He grasped Bronson's hand and slid up through the break in the ceiling in seconds.

The others were gathered together. Caree and Ellie were embracing, and Kendrick was watching them with his hand on Caree's shoulder, looking concerned. Axel was pretty sure one or both of them were crying. Shiznit stood nearby with Uncle Henry, looking like he might be about to faint as the ground rumbled again.

"We need to leave," Bronson said.

Caree pulled back from Ellie and wiped her wet cheeks. "I am so sorry we left you here. I've been so worried." She looked around the group. "I'm sorry… so sorry."

"It's okay." Ellie wiped her eyes. "It's over now," she added. Axel moved toward her.

Kendrick wrapped Caree in his arms. She buried her face in his chest, sobs shaking her with renewed force. Kendrick kissed the top of her head and murmured words too soft for Axel to hear into her hair.

"Oh dear," Uncle Henry said. "Poor Carrot is very upset."

"We've all been through a lot." Axel's throat tightened with the threat of tears of his own. He put his arm around Ellie and drew her close. For once, she didn't pull away. They really hadn't had time to process everything that had happened yet. But they wouldn't have any time at all if they didn't get going to wherever their ride off the planet might be waiting.

As if proving the point, the roof of the corridor buckled and groaned beneath their feet as a new quake shook the ground.

"Okay, kids." Bronson clapped Shiznit on the back so hard the goat-like being lurched forward. "Time to go—"

The ground rumbled, knocking Axel to his knees as the roof they were on swayed dangerously, and the metal sheeting gave way with a loud groaning screech. "Bronson!" Axel shouted. He clutched Ellie close and held on tight while the rumbling gradually subsided.

As the dust settled, it became clear that the portion of the structure that Bronson had been on had collapsed, and the starship captain was no longer visible. Shiznit and Uncle Henry were lying on the roof near the newly broadened opening but seemed otherwise unharmed as they scrambled away from the gap that threatened to swallow them.

"Bronson!" Axel shouted again.

"Oh, shit," Ellie said, her eyes wide.

"I'm okay," Bronson called back, his voice sounding distant.

Kendrick carefully crept toward the edge, Axel following, testing the stressed metal for further weakness. It flexed under their weight but didn't break. Peering over the edge, they could see Bronson standing on the floor below, smacking dust off his long black coat. The length of the corridor they had come through had been ruptured, spilling broken supports and other debris into the opening and narrowing it.

Bronson waved up at them. "I'm fine. You should go," he shouted.

"Stay where you are," Axel shouted. "We'll come down and get you."

"We can move it," Kendrick said, assessing the broken supports with the critical eye of a professional engineer. "But it might make it collapse. Did you bring a rope?" he asked Axel.

"A rope?" Axel stared at his brother. "Yeah, sure. I keep one in my ass for emergencies just like you do."

"You don't have to be sarcastic," Kendrick muttered.

"Oh, no." Caree's voice was soft as she peered over the edge with Ellie.

"Listen," Bronson said. "You guys are all going to die if you don't leave, and that's not the timeline I want to be in. So get your asses moving, will you? Caree knows the way to the cargo ship."

"What?" Ellie asked. "What about you? We can come down and get you. Just give us a moment to figure it out."

"There aren't any moments!" Bronson shouted in a rare expression of true agitation that seemed even more serious in the face of his usual sarcasm. "Don't you see that? You're going to fucking die!"

"But what about you?" Caree asked softly.

"I'll head for the Bohemia."

"You'll never make it." Axel shook his head.

"Neither will you if you don't get going. I'll be fine. I've got tricks up my sleeve you've not even seen yet."

That was something Axel had to agree with. Bronson did seem to be full of secrets and always managed to land on his feet somehow. The ground rumbled, making the roof sway, threatening to tip them all into the hole.

"Just go!" Bronson shouted. "I'll catch up with you later." He turned and started hurrying away from where they were, presumably heading for the Bohemia. *Wherever that was docked,* mused Axel.

The ground shook once again, Henry using Axel to prevent his fall into the hole. "Come on. As I mentioned just moments earlier, we can't wither away our time. Let's do as the gentleman said and make haste!"

"Wither?" Ellie mouthed the word at Axel, looking confused. "Haste?"

Axel shrugged. At least the old man was still thinking. "Let's just go before we can't leave at all." Bronson would have to take his chances. But didn't they all?

Caree's face was scrunched, and she looked miserable at the idea of leaving Bronson behind but took the lead with steady strides, working her way along the roof and avoiding the worst of the places the metal was likely to give way. With the structure unpredictable in its deteriorating state, the best they could muster was quick steps, rather than running, even with Caree's heightened abilities to sense danger.

Axel looked up at the sky. "The air will be unbreathable soon." The clouds were flickering and shimmering as the atmosphere responded to the dimensional flux that was occurring.

"Within the confines of a normal state of affairs, I'd agree. But Amasis is a place where the norm isn't the norm. We will be fine to breathe for as long as there's something still remaining," Henry said, sounding slightly out of breath as he walked as quickly as possible. "We just don't want to be here when Amasis reappears in its new dimension."

"Yes, sounds very bad," Kendrick said, smiling at

Caree like the schoolroom smartass trying to impress the 'hot girl.' In the process, he tripped over a steel pipe jutting from the ground, smashing his shin and landing on his knees with a loud metallic bang. "Shit."

"Kendrick!" Caree shouted, turning mid-stride to see what had happened.

"Get up, bro, you're too frelling big to carry." Axel extended a hand. The group came to an abrupt halt to assist Kendrick. "Can you walk?"

Kendrick grunted as he got to his feet. "I've hurt myself worse mining on planets in the outer rim." He glared at Axel, then smiled upon catching his younger brother's concern and Caree's obvious distress. "But thanks, you little wanker."

Shiznit scratched his head. "What does that word even mean?"

"I'll tell you in private some time," Axel said to the Gho'bar.

The group resumed their trek along the top of the corridor toward the hangar bay, but something was wrong. "Do you feel that?" Axel asked.

"Feel what?" Ellie replied. "I don't feel anything."

"Exactly. The place has stopped trembling. We've been feeling steady rumbles from the quakes since we woke up in the cell and found it obliterated."

Kendrick shrugged. "Well... good. Hopefully, no more surprises on our way to the ship then."

"Must move quicker." Henry darted his way to the front of the group. "Quicker. Quicker!"

"Shit," Axel said. Henry Ryan was a veteran adventurer, and from what Axel knew about his uncle's past exploits, if he was worried, the rest of them should be massively concerned. "It's back building, isn't it?" he called out to his uncle's retreating figure. "The pressure is back building. Are we getting close, Caree?"

She gestured in the direction they were heading. "It's just up ahead. Through the next collapsed section of the roof. Then we're in the hangar where the ship is waiting."

Each step forward was at least half a meter, so two hundred meters at the worst-case scenario. He must have done at least twenty since Caree's assessment, and at any moment, they would be through and at a cargo ship.

A series of blasts, sounding not unlike an electric bandsaw cutting metal girders, filled the air, forcing them to cover their ears. The corridor roof they were hurrying along, which was acting more like a bridge by the second, sagged and tilted to the left, threatening to toss them off into whatever was below. Axel didn't want to wait to find out.

"Move it!" he urged the group.

They ran as fast as they could, each step threatening to destabilize the corridor further. The metal structure shook, sending debris flying in all directions. With visibility dwindling in a cloud of dust and debris, they ran ahead on blind faith alone, ignoring the stinging in their lungs and the cuts caused by sharp edges of metal and stone as the structure started to disintegrate. Roaring thunder filled the air, and Axel didn't even want to guess what more could add to their danger.

"Hold on!" Kendrick screamed as Caree called out in panic.

Axel quickly glanced and stopped in his path. His brother had an arm extended over the edge where Caree dangled precariously, her thin wrist wrapped in his grip.

"Keep going," he urged the others.

He ran to his brother's side. Axel reached for Caree's other wrist as she tried in vain to grab the edge of the roof. Together, they pulled Caree up and over and onto the top.

Kendrick's expression was visibly pinched as he looked at his brother. "I nearly lost her, Axel."

Caree was shaking, her face pale, too overwhelmed to do anything but try to keep breathing. Kendrick picked her up in his arms, carrying her as if she weighed nothing.

"We can't keep doing this much longer," Axel said, panting as they ran toward where the others waited just ahead of them. A deafening roar filled his ears, followed by a wind so strong it pulled at their clothes. They shielded their eyes as they looked up. A large ship came into view above their heads and settled into a hover.

"Axel Ryan, do you copy?" a voice called out through his comm unit.

He didn't immediately recognize the voice or the woman who waved down at them from the open-access port. "Yes." With his lungs protesting the fact he wanted to yell, the one word was about all he could muster.

"Get ready to grab onto the cables. We're going to pull you up."

"This is our ship?" Axel asked Caree.

"Does it matter?" Ellie screamed over the sound of the wind and the protesting groan of the buckling metal beneath their feet. She grabbed the nearest cable as it swung down to her and fastened it to Uncle Henry, making sure Shiznit was attached as well before grabbing one for herself.

"Fucking hurry!" she shouted as she, Shiznit, and Henry disappeared from Axel's hazy view as they were pulled upward and inside the ship. Without a word of warning, three more cables descended in his direction. The pair assisted Caree to one of them, and then both brothers soon gripped one each. "We're on," Axel called through his comm, and with those words, the trio found themselves dragged up and away from the crumbling corridor.

The timing couldn't have been more critical as the moorings gave way and the structure completely collapsed. Within seconds, they were in the cargo vessel's main entry surrounded by a ring of unfamiliar humanoid faces. The dark-skinned woman dressed in a flight suit who had rescued them and seemed to be the one in command stared at each of the recently rescued team members with an unhappy frown.

"Where's Bronson?" she asked.

"We got separated," Caree said, gasping to catch her breath. She leaned against Kendrick as they sagged against the wall for support. Axel joined them, bending forward and leaning his hands onto his knees to catch his breath. "He's gone to the Bohemia instead," Caree added.

"The Bohemia?" the woman asked. "That's where Hendrix went."

"Hendrix is here?" Axel asked.

The woman put up her hand in a gesture of both command and silence. She spoke into her wrist comm. "Hendrix? Do you have Bronson? Hendrix?" Her frown deepened at the lack of reply. "Bronson?" she tried a different comm channel. "Bronson?" she repeated. "Shit." She hissed as the silence continued.

"External comms could be frelled by the flux now," one of the people beside her said.

"We'd better go check." She spoke into her wrist comm again. "Bridge crew, alter course to the Bohemia's last location. We aren't leaving yet."

With a snap of her fingers, she gestured for everyone to follow her out of the main entryway.

"Who are these people?" Axel asked Caree.

"They're the shifters. The last of Hendrix's people," she said and then passed out on Kendrick's chest.

Ellie stood on the bridge of the large cargo vessel that the shifters had dubbed The Maven Haven for whatever reason. Not that it mattered. What did matter was that they were all currently safe. Caree and Phoenix were unconscious in the cargo hold, sleeping off whatever nightmare of exhaustion they had endured, under the watchful eye of the biggest pile of Stardrives Ellie had ever seen. Kendrick and the others had stayed there with them. They all needed to rest, and Shiznit had wanted to be with Marsais, who wouldn't leave Caree and the baby.

Bubbles, however, had insisted on coming to the bridge with Ellie and Axel when she'd realized Bronson had not made it back.

"He's an idiot. He's always been an idiot," the Travanian said while watching the view on the main navigation screen.

"Who? Hendrix or Bronson?" Axel asked. He was

standing slightly behind Ellie and kept trying to drape a blanket around her shoulders.

She shrugged it off again and quickly glanced at him. "Will you please stop that? I'm trying to focus here."

"So am I," the dark-skinned shifter who had introduced herself as Gothani said. She gave them a frown, which Ellie was beginning to think was her normal expression. and turned back to piloting the ship. "This thing flies like a fat goat."

Ellie caught Axel's slight frown. She was glad Shiznit wasn't around right then.

"Well, our goat-friend is a pretty damn good pilot. Maybe you should let him try," Axel said.

"No time to argue," Gothani said. "We're here, and so are they."

Three figures were seen on a section of the ground where once a flat plain might have been, but now it was a jumble of craggy precipices. One of the figures was waving its arms frantically.

"Is that Bronson?" Ellie asked, peering at the viewscreen.

"Looks like." Gothani magnified their view as she banked the ship sharply and swung into a hover position. She called into the shipboard comm, "Drop the cables and bring them on board. We don't have time to linger."

Bubbles disappeared to help with the rescue. Ellie stared at the viewscreen, Axel beside her.

"But who's that with him?"

Bronson grabbed the cables that were lowered down to him, but the other two figures were lying on the ground, not moving. He carefully hooked them up and made sure they were fastened securely before securing his own and signaling to be pulled up.

"It's Remler and T-183." Axel looked grim as he watched the three ascend and disappear through the doorway onboard.

"Are they hurt?" Ellie asked. The two Bohemia crewmates hadn't moved a muscle while rising through the air.

"Who knows," Gothani said in her droll voice. "Let's rescue them first and find out, shall we?"

"There's no ship," Axel pointed out. "The Bohemia is gone."

"Yes," Gothani agreed. "You guys really like stating the obvious, don't you?"

"So what happened to Hendrix?" Ellie asked.

"Hendrix is gone," Bronson announced, sounding out of breath. He strode onto the bridge at a fast pace, Bubbles hot on his heels. "He took the Bohemia and left T-183 and Remler with me."

"Wha—" Ellie began, but Bronson cut her off with a quick raise of his hand.

"No time to explain right now. We need to get out of here like yesterday." He glanced at the controls of the ship quickly. "Bubbles, you take co-pilot.

Gothani? I'm going to drive. Thanks for coming back for me, but we need to let the professionals take it from here now, yeah? Axel, thanks, my friend. Very thoughtful of you." He grabbed the blanket out of Axel's hands and tossed it around his shoulders, at which point Ellie realized that Bronson wasn't wearing his signature long black coat. What the frell had happened to him in the short time they had been apart?

As Bubbles and Bronson took their positions, Bronson turned to Gothani. "No, no, you don't need to leave the bridge with a grumpy face. We need you to help navigate. This ship doesn't happen to have temporal shielding, does it?" He scanned the controls quickly, not waiting for Gothani's response as she took over the position as navigator, relieving the shifter who had been sitting there. It was interesting, Ellie mused, that they had all chosen to take on human form. Maybe it was easier to control a ship like this that was designed for humanoids. "No?" Bronson surmised. "Didn't think so. Remler will need to be kept sedated then. He doesn't do well unshielded." He gestured at his head with his hands. "All the multiple realities make him a bit unstable."

"What about T-183?" Ellie asked.

"Eh?" Bronson turned to look at her. "Oh, she'll be fine once she reboots." He turned back to the console and adjusted the controls, angling the ship toward the sky once more.

"But what—" Axel began.

"No time, no time," Bronson said. "This planet is literally about to blow. The Stardrives were the last thing holding it together, and now most of them are onboard our ship. It's like a big bomb, you know?" He turned back to face them as the ship hit the cloud layer. "By the way, you might want to strap yourselves in. Things are going to get bumpy, and we can't slow down now, or we won't make it."

The ship began to vibrate as the turbulence within the clouds increased. Axel and Ellie took the only vacant seats left on the bridge in the gunner area. Why a cargo ship like this would need weapons was a good question, but maybe it had been a runner in its day.

The turbulence increased as they traveled toward the upper atmosphere, causing the ship's hull to groan under the stress. Ellie was beginning to wonder if her teeth might rattle out of her head. "What about the others in the cargo hold?" she called out, raising her voice to be heard above the noise.

"The Stardrives will protect them," Bronson said. His grip on the wheel was strained as he struggled to maintain control of the ship. "I'm hoping they'll protect the whole ship, or once we hit that chronotron barrier, this will be a pretty short trip."

"You mean you don't know what's going to

happen?" Ellie shouted as the rattling and noise became almost unbearable.

"No," Bronson said.

"What? Why not? I thought you were a time traveler. Don't you know everything?"

"Sometimes I don't want to." Bronson grinned back at her. "Makes it more interesting that way."

"Oh, my God!" Ellie cried out. "He's gone crazy!"

Ellie buried her face in Axel's shoulder as he reached to hold her and pressed his face into her hair. The viewscreen was filled with a bright flash of light so brilliant it filled the entire bridge. It seemed for a long second like light, sound, and movement all stopped, and they floated in nothingness. Then they were through the chronotron barrier that surrounded Amasis and back into the void of regular space.

"Are we alive?" Ellie whispered, not daring to open her eyes and trust her vision yet. After the day they'd been through with so many close calls, she didn't want to tempt fate.

"I think so." Axel's breath was warm and uneven against the top of her head. As he pulled away, she felt him tense. "Oh shit," he said.

"No, no," Ellie said, keeping her eyes shut tight as renewed despair set in. "You're supposed to say everything's good. Not, oh shit."

She didn't want to see whatever it was. If she kept her eyes closed, it wasn't real. Right? With a sigh, she opened her eyes and then wished she hadn't. "Oh, shit," she said.

Bronson, Bubbles, Gothani, and everyone else appeared to have passed out from the stress of the trip through the barrier. But maybe that was a good thing because at least they didn't have to see the entire fleet of Core ships that the Maven was slowly drifting toward.

"This is Commander Ortega of the Core battle cruiser, Rehnquist. Surrender at once and prepare to be boarded."

Thank you for reading Core Shifter.

Coming Soon

Lost Legacy

Other Books in the Series

Queen Killer Book 1
Star Keeper Book 2
Dark Horizon Book 3

Fatal Fortress Book 3
Phoenix Rising Book 5

Find more stories from Chris Heinicke and Kate Reedwood at www.legacyhunter.space

Coming soon in the Legacy Hunter Universe
The Galactic Misfits Series

ACKNOWLEDGMENTS

Thank you to the internet gods for creating a world where two people can live on opposite sides of the planet, be fourteen, fifteen, sixteen hours out of sync in time, (thanks to daylight savings as well, haha), and still write books together.

Thank you to Glenda and Mike for understanding our need to write this sixth story together and the constant hours of conversations that engendered.

Thank you to Alex for all your fantastic ideas concerning Stardrives and Borbs and your constant enthusiasm for us writing this story.

Thank you to Ethan, Krystal, and Siobhan for being the most amazing children and letting Daddy write during those moments between reattaching doll legs, giving you cuddles, food, and love, and working crazy, crazy hours.

Thank you to Swish Design & Editing for your excellent editing and formatting assistance, Nicole Ulery for being one hell of a personal assistant, and Ash Madi and Jarrod Elvin for bringing the characters to life in art form.

Thank you to our readers and the members of the Legacy Hunter Guild for all your support, especially our beta reader team, Kat, Kate, Pat, and Suzanne, for your feedback.

Special thanks to Sharon for 'Nigel' the alien, and to the members of the Legacy Hunter Guild for your assistance in naming the Visitors homeworld as well as many other planets and extraterrestrial species in this series.

Join the Legacy Hunter Guild

https://www.facebook.com/groups/1812276449059713/

Get Legacy Hunter News Directly in your Inbox

https://subscribepage.com/kcstories

Website

https://www.legacyhunter.space/

CONNECT WITH US ONLINE

KC STORIES

Find our exciting stories at:
https://www.legacyhunter.space

LEGACY HUNTER

FACEBOOK
https://www.facebook.com/LegacyHunterSeries

INSTAGRAM
https://www.instagram.com/legacyhunterseries/

READER GROUP

Want access to fun, prizes and sneak peeks?
Join our Facebook Reader Group.
https://www.facebook.com/groups/1812276449059713/

NEWSLETTER

https://subscribepage.com/kcstories

WEBSITE

https://www.legacyhunter.space/

EMAIL

KCBooks@LegacyHunter.space

POST

KC Stories Canada
200 North Service Road West,
Suite 936
Oakville, ON L6M 2Y1
CANADA

KC Stories Australia
49 Combine Street
Coffs Harbour, NSW 2450
AUSTRALIA

AUTHORS

Follow the Authors on Social Media:

CHRIS HEINICKE

FACEBOOK

https://www.facebook.com/ChrisHeinickeWriter

INSTAGRAM

https://www.instagram.com/heinickewriter/

AMAZON

https://www.amazon.com/
Chris-Heinicke/e/B00TIHKF4M

GOODREADS

https://www.goodreads.com/author/show/
13494100.Chris_Heinicke

KATE REEDWOOD

FACEBOOK

https://www.facebook.com/KateReedwood

INSTAGRAM

https://www.instagram.com/katereedwood/

AMAZON

https://www.amazon.com/
Kate-Reedwood/e/B071FVTHNW

GOODREADS

https://www.goodreads.com/author/show/1419
1256.Kate_Reedwood

BOOKBUB

https://www.bookbub.com/profile/k-reedwood

ABOUT THE AUTHORS

CHRIS HEINICKE

Although working as a baker for many years, writing has been a passion for Chris for some time, starting in high school and reigniting again in 2006, when he first got the inspiration to begin writing *The Man In Black*. After completing that project eight years later, he took part in NaNoWriMo in November 2014, culminating in a project named 5PM. Deciding to self-publish, *5PM* came out in February 2015, and then *The Man In Black* in August.

2016 saw the release of *7PM*, and in that same year, his writing path met with that of Canadian author, Kate Reedwood. A mutual respect for each other's work ignited an interest in working together, creating the Legacy Hunter series, the first of which came out in July 2017.

Apart from writing, Chris enjoys traveling, reading, watching movies, and all things geeky. He resides in Coffs Harbour with his wife and three children.

KATE REEDWOOD

Kate Reedwood, also known as Felicity Kates, is a mild-mannered manager by day. At night, she trades in her high heels for bunny slippers and lets her imagination run wild.

A trained artist and writer, Kate enjoys writing stories that combine humor with strong characters who know what they want and aren't afraid to go get it. Every story is an emotional journey where the characters must struggle to find their happily ever after. But they do always reach it in the end, no matter the time or place in the universe.

She lives off coffee and dreams and enjoys going for walks along the shores of Lake Ontario, taking pictures of whatever catches her eye. A romantic at heart, she loves to snuggle under a blanket with a good book to warm up the cold Canadian winters.

When not dreaming up new worlds and books to write with Australian author, Chris Heinicke, she can most often be found enjoying the quiet company of her husband and son.

You can stay up to date with Chris and Kate at:
https://www.legacyhunter.space/

Manufactured by Amazon.ca
Bolton, ON

22617745R00142